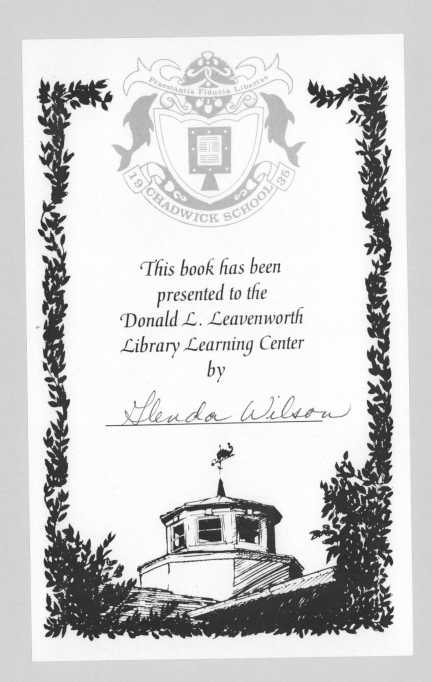

Praestantia Fiducia Libertas

19 CHADWICK SCHOOL 35

This book has been
presented to the
Donald L. Leavenworth
Library Learning Center
by

Glenda Wilson

A GARDEN FOR CHILDREN

Also by Felicity Bryan:

The Town Gardener's Companion

A GARDEN FOR CHILDREN

BY

FELICITY BRYAN

WATERCOLOURS BY ELISABETH LUARD

MICHAEL JOSEPH
LONDON

For Alice and Maxim

First published in Great Britain by Michael Joseph Ltd
44 Bedford Square, London WC1
1986

© Felicity Bryan 1986
© colour illustrations Elisabeth Luard 1986
© line drawings Wendy Bramall 1986

Bryan, Felicity
    A Garden for children.
    1. Children's gardens
    I. Title   II. Luard, Elisabeth
    790.1'922   SB457

    ISBN 0 7181 2580 0

Filmset by BAS Printers Limited, Over Wallop, Hampshire
Printed and bound in Italy by A. Mondadori

CONTENTS

Acknowledgements 6

Why have a garden? 7

Designing your garden for children 15

Plans for family gardens 27

How does your garden grow? 51

Starting to garden 69

A garden of your own 87

Some children's gardens 105

Secret gardens 115

Miniature gardens 127

Your garden nature reserve 143

Safety in the garden 163

Indoor jobs for a rainy day 173

Your garden calendar 185

Bibliography 189

Index 190

ACKNOWLEDGEMENTS

A Garden for Children has been fun to write because I have had so much help and enthusiasm from other people. Jennie Davies at Michael Joseph has been an ideal editor: keen, tactful and fun. Her energy certainly rubbed off on her assistant Michèle Young, who is both efficient and most encouraging, and on the excellent designer Susan McIntyre. It was Jennie who selected the illustrators Elisabeth Luard (for the colour paintings) and Wendy Bramall (for the black and white drawings) whose entrancing work transformed the book giving it a whole life of its own.

For help in writing the book, I am particularly grateful to Daniel Russell and his daughter Suzy. He designed the very imaginative garden plans, she gave me plans for her own garden and together they read through my text and came up with many original suggestions. Anthony Leatham and his daughters Caroline and Jennifer kindly told me of all their fascinating experiments with plants, which are an exciting addition, and both children allowed me to write about their gardens. My thanks also to Augustin Glazebrook and Toby Baring for showing me their gardens.

On the home front David, Adam and Kieran Evans have constantly given me new ideas and Karen Hilsden has made it all possible by cheerfully looking after my children while I wrote. Lastly, my husband Alex Duncan has encouraged and helped me all along and it is he and our children Alice and Maxim who provided the inspiration for this book.

WHY HAVE A GARDEN

'Oh! the things which happened in that garden! If you have never had a garden, you cannot understand, and if you have had a garden, you will know that it would take a whole book to describe all that came to pass there.'

THE SECRET GARDEN

WHY HAVE A GARDEN

Do you know the story of the Selfish Giant? If not, you have missed something. The story goes like this: the Giant returned from a long visit to his friend the Ogre to find the children playing in his garden. He was angry and turned them out and put up a sign saying 'Trespassers will be prosecuted'. And so things might have remained. But the garden went on protest strike. 'The birds did not care to sing in it as there were no children, and the trees forgot to blossom. Once a beautiful flower put its head out from the grass, but when it saw the notice board it was so sorry for the children that it slipped back into the ground again, and went off to sleep. The only people who were pleased were the Snow and the Frost.' So winter remained in the garden when all outside was spring.

The Giant finally changed his mind when he saw a wonderful sight. 'Through a little hole in the wall the children had crept in, and they were sitting in the branches of the trees. In every tree that he could see there was a little child. And the trees were so glad to have the children back again that they had covered themselves with blossoms, and were waving their arms gently above the children's heads. The birds were flying about and twittering with delight, and the flowers were looking up through the green grass and laughing.' So the Giant became their friend and in the end it was the tiny boy whom he helped up a tree who welcomed him in heaven.

The reason that Oscar Wilde's romantic children's story still moves me is that it links children and gardens in a way that I think is right. Children and gardens should go hand in hand, for a garden needs children as much as they need it. A garden may be beautifully kept and trimmed, but if it has no place for fun and games and adventure, then it lacks an essential life. And there is no reason why a garden that has space and place for children should not be beautiful and interesting for adults at the same time. I actually prefer gardens that are rather wild and full of surprises, where it looks as if nature has only been slightly tamed – and so do children.

Throughout children's literature you find stories in which the really exciting events – often the magic ones – happen in the garden. This is particularly so in Victorian and Edwardian stories like *The Secret Garden* or *Alice in Wonderland*. Alice looks through the tiny door and sees 'the loveliest garden you ever saw' and that is when her adventures begin.

More recently, in that glorious book *Tom's Midnight Garden*, Tom is forced to go and stay with unexciting adults in a flat in an old house which has no garden. He is miserable until he discovers that when everyone else is asleep and the clock strikes thirteen, the garden which used to exist comes back to life. He is taken back in time and has wonderfully mysterious adventures with a little girl called Hatty who is almost killed climbing one of the many huge trees which make the garden so exciting. In due course Tom's nighttime life comes to seem more real than the day : 'The garden was the thing. That was real.'

In Victorian times the children of wealthy parents must have found the large gardens of their homes a marvellous escape from the strict disciplines that existed indoors. There were shrubberies, orchards, huge greenhouses and all sorts of secret places where their imaginations could run free. Tom was quite surprised to see how thrilled Hatty was by their tree house which she thought of as 'her own house and home, and she talked wildly of furnishing it with her doll's tea set and even with objects filched from the spare bedrooms in the big house . . . she had made this garden a kind of kingdom'. And Mary in *The Secret Garden* had just the same new feeling of independence from the world of grown-ups once she found her garden.

Of course most children today have much greater freedom and most of our gardens are not nearly as big as those I have described. But this does not mean that children will not derive every bit as much pleasure from a garden as Hatty and Mary did. So the purpose of this book is to suggest many ways in which you can make your own garden more fun and interesting for both parents and children while keeping it a delight to look at. And it seems sensible to start by listing what I feel are the great benefits of a garden and gardening for children.

To start with the obvious, gardens are the most marvellous places to play. As a child I lived on a farm and we had a good-sized garden with an orchard and rough shrubby area as well as the formal lawn and flower-beds. We had swings and trapezes; we built tree houses; we made dens; we played endless ball games and different varieties of hide-and-seek; and, best of all, we had our own little gardens. When it rained we mucked about in the wendy house or the potting shed. Altogether I was very lucky. But even a small garden can contain many of the ingredients for hours of entertainment.

A garden is also a place of fantasy: in wendy houses, tree houses and dens children can create a whole world of their own. In so many children's stories, it is in the garden that the magic happens. In Mary's secret garden she felt, 'The garden had reached the time when every day and every night it seemed as if Magicians were passing through it', and the more you can shape your garden to leave mysterious nooks and crannies and secret areas, the more fun the children will have. My sister and I planted a fairy ring of tiny daffodils. By now it has lost its shape and the daffodils have spread widely but it is still there as a witness to our childhood dreams.

And a garden is very much a place for learning, for children and adults alike. For a start, by making your garden as appealing as possible to birds, insects and animals and observing them close at hand, you will learn an incredible amount about nature. You will also have the opportunity to find out about plants and their changing life cycles.

I have noticed that even in the course of Easter egg hunts and treasure hunts children can't help but look closely at the plants around them and, with your assistance, they may well enjoy learning how to grow both flowers and vegetables. There are numerous experiments using plants that will teach them a good deal about chemistry and, if you keep rain gauges and thermometers, they can learn about how the weather works as well. Then on, perhaps, to making things in the garden, starting with sandpits and graduating as they get older to more complicated earthworks, bird-boxes and -tables, and furniture for the den.

Children's memories are amazing. They learn poems and songs with an ease that takes your breath away. As they grow up that capacity will go, so grasp the moment. We used to have a competition at school to see who could identify and remember the names of a hundred wild flowers. I remember my enthusiasm for it and one year, when I was nine, I got the lot right. The nice legacy of this story is that I still remember nearly all of them whereas names I learn today don't stick in the same way.

The names of garden plants can tell you a lot about their origins and as children get older they may develop an interest in garden history, in the fascinating stories of how individual plants were discovered in such faraway places as China, India and South America and brought to the west by daring explorers. In the eighteenth century John Bartram explored the American west when it was still very wild and introduced over a hundred species to Europe, while in the nineteenth century George Forrest braved the dangerous valleys of Tibet and China, later bringing back with him over three hundred species of rhododendron.

But there are other, less tangible, things to be learned in a garden. I have no doubt, for example, that gardening teaches you patience. Most children are naturally impatient and in the early gardening days they will probably pull up seeds to see how they are getting on. They have to learn to attune themselves to nature's cycles, to be prepared to wait. But having said this, I also think that adults can learn a lot from children's very impulsive, fresh approach to plants and gardens which can somehow temper their own more rational – but usually less inspired – ideas.

I also think that gardening teaches you about sharing, for so much that is done involves joint efforts and giving things – whether it is sharing your seeds or taking cuttings, or collaborating on a little flower-bed. In her charming book *A Flat Iron for a Farthing*, published in 1884, Mrs Julia Horatia Ewing's young hero Reginald is told by his old gardening mentor Mr Andrewes, 'If ever you see anybody with a good garden full of flowers who grudges picking them for his friends, you may be quite sure he has not learnt half of what flowers can teach him. Flowers are generous enough. The more you take from them the more they give.'

Towards the end of this book I have included a chapter on safety in the garden and I think it very important, but I do also believe that children should learn how to look after themselves and each other in the garden. It is an ideal place for them to learn how to respect other people's things, not to mention nature itself.

But lastly it is the place where parents and children can have a lovely time together, whether they are playing games or are involved in a joint enterprise like building a tree house or starting a vegetable patch. When

you plan your garden you should definitely involve the children in the decision-making. Get them to draw wonderful ground plans and they are bound to come up with some imaginative – if sometimes impractical – thoughts. This sharing cannot but cheer up family life, as Mrs Ewing observed. Once a child is of a certain age and can take a real interest in gardening the age gap seems irrelevant: looking back, Reginald remembers, 'Mr Andrewes had already fired my imagination with dreams of a little garden in perfect order and beauty, and tended by my own hands alone; and as I talked of my garden, the parson talked of his, and so we wandered from border to border, finding each other very good company.'

Of course, at different ages children will enjoy different things. At three they may start to weed and sow simple seeds, but it is unlikely that children will become seriously interested in gardening before the age of six. From then on it can be a growing and continuing interest into their early teens when suddenly it tends to stop. Other exciting attractions take over and weekends are devoted instead to football games, parties and fun with friends away from home.

But don't be disheartened. Once you have loved gardening I think it is always there – a little flame waiting to be refuelled at the right time. With me it happened when I bought my first house. It had a long, narrow garden which I set about transforming with a pergola over the terrace, tubs galore, a herb garden and flower beds. I made it very private by growing all kinds of climbing roses and honeysuckle so it became my own secret garden in the heart of London. And I remember thinking that the sheer thrill and excitement that I experienced seeing my changes take effect made me feel like a child again. And that, perhaps, is the secret of why we like to garden.

DESIGNING YOUR GARDEN FOR CHILDREN

'Reka Dom in a remarkable degree answered our requirements. To explore the garden was like a tour in fairy land. It was oddly laid out. Three grass plots or lawns, one behind another, were divided by hedges of honeysuckle . . . . And what a place for bowers!'

REKA DOM. from *Mrs Overtheway's Remembrances*

DESIGNING YOUR GARDEN FOR CHILDREN

MY daughter Alice is lucky enough to have a summer birthday, so her party is always held in the garden. On her second birthday all the children arrived kitted out so prettily, but within minutes the frilly dresses were thrown aside and ten children were in the paddling pool. By tea time none of them was wearing anything but a paper hat. They required no entertainment: the combination of a good lawn, swings, a hammock and the paddling pool plus odd toys was quite enough. There were no tears. Everyone was relaxed. The garden *made* her party a success.

From the moment when a child first crawls on to the lawn to when he or she holds teenage barbecues, the garden can be the most pleasurable room in your home. But to make it work well requires some thoughtful planning. In later chapters I give some design suggestions, but to start with it is worth thinking about the ingredients that make up a successful garden for children. Obviously requirements change with the ages of your children and you don't want to sacrifice beauty entirely, but there is still an enormous amount you can do.

I must point out that when I refer to a garden I mean the whole area outside your house that belongs to you including the part around the garage and what in America is called the back yard.

THE TERRACE OR PATIO

Toddlers are into everything. They have no sense of danger and are generally fearless, so they must be supervised at all times. Yet at the same time you want them to explore on their own and develop a sense of independence.

17

The only way that busy parents can combine these requirements is by situating the toddlers' area of garden close to the house so that you can keep an eye on the children while doing something else. Just outside the kitchen is ideal. We luckily have a big kitchen with an indoor play area just beside the French windows into the garden. So the children can wander in and out and I can watch while working there.

Ideally the area outside should be paved so that children can play there with their bicycles, trucks of bricks and anything else on wheels as well as balls. It will also dry out more quickly after rain and can be kept clean quite easily. As such, it also suits the needs of the adults in the family as it offers a perfect space for outdoor eating.

This is such a pleasure for all ages that these days there aren't many families who haven't set aside a space for a barbecue. While it is possible to buy a portable barbecue, such as a habachi, if you have enough room think of building one in an attractive stone or brick or whatever goes best with your house.

We also built a low stone wall around our terrace. It is wide and flat-topped so that adults can sit on it comfortably, but equally it acts as a kind of barrier and there is a gate that can be put across the entrance on to the lawn. Don't be afraid to make this area quite large. With pretty tubs and flowers growing on the wall it will look very full and attractive – and the more space toddlers have, the better.

In summer the terrace is a good place for a portable plastic wendy house. All children love to hide from grown-ups and have a place of their own to which they can invite their friends, so this is extremely popular. In the winter it can live in a child's bedroom.

LAWNS

With children, the more space you have for lawn the better. There they can play all kinds of games and generally romp about. Don't hanker after a bowling green or you will be disappointed. Instead lay turf or sow seed of a tough grass mixture containing rye grass as this will stand up to much more wear and tear. If you move to a new house with no decent lawn, lay turf right away: it would be stupid to sow seed and have to wait a year for a useable lawn, and you would only end up with mud in the house and frustrated children.

Though you want the lawn to be big enough for games, do your best when laying it out to leave areas of mystery – the lawn might flow down behind some shrubs or trees, for example – so that there is shelter for hide-and-seek and other activities. Obviously this is not easy with a tiny garden but always bear in mind that element of surprise which children love.

FLOWER-BEDS

Don't think that because there are children about you should abandon the idea of flower-beds. Children are fascinated by flowers and it is your job to teach them to respect them. However, there are certain common-sense precautions you should take.

When we moved house our new front lawn was criss-crossed with rectangular rose beds. Our first job was to get rid of all the roses (they were replanted elsewhere) and turf over the beds. 'Island' beds just don't make sense with children about, so keep flower-beds to the sides of the lawn but make them interesting shapes and make sure they are large enough for some good planting.

In a small garden or on a patio you might build raised beds of brick. These are expensive but can be extremely attractive and they have the advantage of being at the eye-level of smaller children, so are fun for them.

Then of course there are the children's own flower-beds. If you have the space it would be a dreadful shame not to give the children a flower-bed of their own and follow up with every encouragement you can. In later chapters I write about this in detail but remember to keep the beds quite small so that the children will not become discouraged early. And see that they are in a nice sunny spot with easy access to water so that the plants have the best chance of survival.

Given the chance, a child would probably opt for a garden that he or she could tend alone rather than share with brothers and sisters or friends. But in fact a shared garden stands a better chance of looking pretty and not suffering from lack of attention. If you don't have room for individual beds you might allocate a particular area of the garden or even a garden trough or tub that is specially theirs. Miniature gardens can be enormously popular too.

PLACES TO PLAY

The more natural play places your garden has, the better.

Trees are important to any garden, but with children mature trees can be a special boon. From the branches you can hang swings, ropes, trapezes, hammocks, rings and ladders which will keep them happy for hours. If you have several trees, hang bird-feeders from branches and attach bird-boxes and bat-boxes to the trunks, but keep the bird-boxes away from the centre of the children's activity area or the birds will take fright and leave. The greatest excitement is a tree house and this need not be a complicated affair. When I was small our 'house' was in fact no more than a wooden deck firmly nailed on top of two adjacent branches, with some kind of awning rigged up if we felt so inclined. But obviously if you are keen on do-it-yourself the possibilities of palaces in the air are enormous. Just be very sure that the branches are safe, for however much your heart is in your mouth it is impossible to stop children climbing trees. Your job is to make it as safe as possible by cutting away the rotting, unstable branches and pruning those dangerous jagged stumps left where branches have broken off.

A German lady once described a mulberry tree as 'kinderfreundlich' – friendly to children – and I thought of that description when I visited a friend with a weeping mulberry tree. In summer the large leaves make it impossible to see through and so it forms a natural tent for her grandchildren to play in. We have a swing hanging on ours. In autumn, our children love to eat the purple berries, but a word of warning – if you value your carpets watch out for the stains brought into the house by little feet.

Hedges are another great source of fun. Old evergreen hedges of box or yew make marvellous dens and are great places for hide-and-seek. You can create secret places with little screens of fast-growing conifers but be careful not to disturb the birds which love to nest there. Hedges can also

20

be used to separate off the adults' more private area.

Then there are man-made play places. Children enjoy **sandpits** from the moment they can first sit up on their own. You can have quite a rough one made in a shallow hole in the ground with wooden stockading to keep the shape, or you can be more elaborate. A square, rectangular, round or octagonal sandpit built of bricks or stone can look very good and might later become a flower-bed or pool when the children are older.

If you can, make a sandpit cover to protect the sand from becoming dirtied with leaves, cat droppings etc., and to keep out the rain. A wooden one would mean that the sandpit could double as a table or seat when not in use. And remember not to use builders' sand as it stains and does not dry out so well. Special sharp sand drains better and is more attractive. It is a good idea to have a low table or bench beside the sandpit on which children can turn out their sandcastles.

A development from the sandpit is a larger kind of earthworks, probably consisting of a mixture of sand and earth. My cousin's children have built one in a rather secluded area at the side of their suburban house, so it does not matter if it looks a dreadful mess. Here the children make streams and dams of ever increasing complexity and generally muck about for hours on end.

Swings. No garden should be without a swing. By the time she was a year old my daughter was ready for her first one, with a safety bar across and a strap to tie her in. Later comes the traditional short plank or the old car tyre and later still the trapeze. Eventually children can do quite hair-raising things on swings so be sure they are not hung on a concrete area. Stick to grass, if you can.

Hammocks are also enormous fun. We have rather an elaborate one brought back for us from Brazil: it is pretty, soft and comfortable and the children love it. You can easily buy a simple strong string one which, if treated, can live outdoors – bring it in in winter – or you can make one with rope and strong canvas.

Climbing frames were not part of my childhood and I plainly missed a lot. They are wonderful things. There is no end to the variety of activities you can initiate with a climbing frame or jungle jim. Swings, rope ladders, scrambling nets and ropes can hang from them; slides can be attached to them. And you can create all kinds of obstacles to add to the fun. A large climbing frame might have a high play deck or an enclosed stockaded area where children can play house, or there could be walkways made of car tyres strung together. Car tyres can be put to so many imaginative uses – nine attached in three lines of three to form a square with one in the middle make an entertaining extension for any climbing frame.

Aluminium frames can be bought to assemble in your garden. These have the advantage of being weatherproof but there are better-looking small wooden ones which can also be used indoors. Much more attractive are the ones made from sturdy natural logs. But remember that they must be regularly painted or treated with wood preservative or they will begin to rot and become dangerous.

The great attraction of designing your own climbing frame is that no two are alike. You need tall log posts, thinner wood for ladders, ropes and maybe chains. Before you begin, look at the climbing frames in local playgrounds to get some ideas. I took detailed photographs of lots of frames before we began. And don't attempt to build one yourself unless you are very experienced. If you are not, enlist the help of a carpenter. It's important that the main supporting poles should be well secured several feet deep in the ground with cement at the base, and they should be treated with wood preservative before you start.

I have seen climbing frames painted brilliant shades of red and green, blue and yellow. Somehow I think these colours look more appropriate in a town garden or at the seaside. If you are going to live with the frame for a long time, I think a natural wood is a better choice. One thing I would like to see is a climbing frame attached to a tree so the two could, so to speak, integrate and children could scramble from one to the other.

See-saws are not that difficult to make, but again take expert advice before you risk your children's limbs. All you need is a base of some kind – traditionally a thick log – a plank smoothed clear of any splinters and some pieces of wood to attach to the plank. These should be attached to the underside on either side of the base so the plank cannot slip off-centre. Then attach a larger piece of wood near to each end of the plank which the children can hold on to and will stop them sliding forward. Some modern kits have see-saws that double up as slides.

Slides are fun from an early age. Our neighbours have a small plastic one that can be used indoors and is great fun in summer when combined

22

with a paddling pool. Other good ideas are attaching a slide to a tree so you can climb up and slide down, or fixing a slide on a steep slope and making steps up the side out of logs.

Small children seem to love playing in **tunnels**. In one playground I visited I saw a piece of drainage pipe about two feet in diameter and six feet long which had been laid at the base of a climbing frame. It seemed very popular indeed. We have an old water butt without its bottom which serves a similar purpose. You can also buy plastic tunnels and barrels.

Obviously, if you have plenty of space there are many more garden toys which, with a bit of imagination, you can devise yourself. We are currently in the process of mounting an old boat on a stable base – a magnificent play area. Wooden animals, even the most basic ones made from a couple of logs, are very popular. Then an exciting, albeit expensive, addition is a trampoline. If you can't run to this, a couple of old sprung mattresses can be fun if you have somewhere to store them under cover.

Garden houses of all sorts are another great source of delight. They need not be too expensive, made of old orange boxes, perhaps, with corrugated plastic on the top. There's a model to suit every pocket. However, it is worth taking the trouble to build a really nice wendy house as later on children can sleep there in the summer when their friends come to stay. Tents are useful for the same purpose and are also marvellous for games. If you don't want to buy one, you can make a makeshift wigwam.

Finally, you need some **flat surfaces**, both on the ground and on walls, for ball games, for practising tennis, and for roller-skating.

In American gardens a basketball hoop is an essential, though the British equivalent, a netball goal, is less popular. Other good garden games are volleyball and of course croquet – a wonderful family game for older children and adults. We have specially made our lawn large enough for croquet and children from about the age of eight upwards seem to love it. If your lawn has bumps, it makes it all the more interesting.

WATER

Children adore water in all forms. In summer, in our terrace area we have a cheap inflatable plastic paddling pool and it gives endless pleasure. It is important not to have permanent pools when toddlers are about as they can easily drown in very shallow water. Always empty your paddling pool when it is not in use and never leave a toddler near it unattended.

Once children are old enough for it not to be dangerous, a garden pond teeming with fish and wildlife will provide untold excitement. If you can afford it, a swimming pool will provide even greater entertainment, particularly if you live somewhere that has long, hot summers. But looking after a pool is quite time-consuming, and of course it is advisable not to instal one until the children can swim. For younger children, you can buy small free-standing plastic swimming pools which are fun, but again you must be around to supervise.

I have friends who make a temporary pool for children's parties and I am longing to try it myself. They get hay bales from a nearby farm, form the shape they want, then take a huge sheet of thick polythene (bought easily and cheaply from a building supplier) and line the shape. They then fill it with water using the garden hose and there is an instant pool.

Running water is always intriguing and my children are particularly fascinated by fountains. We have a friend who commissioned one from a local sculptor. It has four frogs sitting round a pool with small jets of water coming out of their mouths. In a small space you could have a wall fountain, with water spouting from a bizarre stone face. Fountains with little electric pumps are easy to instal and I highly recommend them.

ORNAMENT

Garden ornaments can provide such a lot of fun and interest. While garden gnomes may not appeal, statues of all sorts can be found if you keep your eyes open and children love them. We have a charming Chinese goddess I bought in a junk shop, our neighbours have some stone animals, and down the road there is a windmill – and so on. Think about putting a sundial on a plinth which the children can read, or building a bird-bath or bird-table, or make a mobile or some windchimes. All of these features are extremely popular and look delightful.

Topiary, the art of cutting evergreen shrubs into shapes, is another amazing form of garden ornament. When I was a child there was an old man in our village who had a yew hedge with peacocks, foxes, rabbits and squirrels carved out of the yew running along the top. We simply loved it. Topiary is obviously quite a skill and takes years to develop. You need to form a frame for the shape you have in mind, using perhaps on old wire coat hanger or some garden wire, and grow the yew around it. Yew is satisfying as it grows quite fast. Box, the best shrub for topiary, is so slow-growing that you would not have that teddy bear or pigeon shape until your children had left home. For the very quickest results try common privet (*Ligustrum ovalifolium*) which has the additional advantage of coming in green- and golden-leaved varieties. It grows very fast and will give you your shape in a couple of years. However, you will have to keep clipping very regularly to keep the required shape.

ANIMALS

Both domestic and wild animals are very much a part of garden life. Many pets can live in hutches outdoors for all but the coldest months of the year, depending of course on where you live. Before you choose your pet, however, take advice from the local petshop which should have an idea of what you can keep in your area.

Rabbits are enormous fun and in summer you can create a large run, giving them a lot of freedom. Guinea pigs are easy to look after and can live in hutches outside for the summer. If you have the space, you might decide to keep bantams or chickens. There are numerous varieties to choose from, including the Polish bantams which appear to wear funny feathered hats. Geese vary in temperament and again you should take advice, though I am told that Pilgrim geese are very good-natured.

Children can be put in charge of feeding any of these animals, but you will always have to check that they are taking their responsibilities seriously. I was brought up on a farm and think I had the best childhood imaginable, so I hope to create a mini-farm for our children. Water birds like ducks are marvellous if you have a good-sized pond. We also keep white pigeons which are pretty but they do breed at an amazing rate and tend to devour the young vegetables in the garden. Be warned!

These are just some of the ingredients that go to make a successful garden for children. No doubt you will think of many more. For invention is all part of the game.

PLANS FOR FAMILY GARDENS

*'A great lawn where flower-beds bloomed; a towering fir
tree, and thick beetle-browed yews that humped their
shapes down two sides of the lawn; on the third side, to
the right, a greenhouse almost the size of a real house;
from each corner of the lawn, a path that twisted away
to some other depths of garden, with other trees.'*

TOM'S MIDNIGHT GARDEN

PLANS FOR FAMILY GARDENS

NO two gardens are exactly alike, so when you set out to design a garden to suit the whole family you should first look around and see what natural features you have that might be incorporated. With luck there will be an old tree with wide spreading branches, a number of mature shrubs, a natural pool, and so on.

So the following ten plans, which I have worked out with a garden designer who has children of his own, are not meant to be followed studiously. They are intended more as sources of ideas. We have chosen lots of very different situations from a balcony to a large suburban garden, though we have put more emphasis on smaller gardens where the challenges and problems are that much greater. But in all of the plans, the idea is to combine comfort and beauty for the adults with lots of excitement and entertainment for the children. Of course, these things overlap all the time: children can become interested in pretty flowers at an early age and watching birds on a bird-table never loses its fascination to older people. It's never too early to train a conservationist, so all the gardens have places for birds and insects to live and feed and the larger ones have special wild areas.

The plans also attempt to show how a garden can be modified as the children get older. For instance, we illustrate a large variety of sandpits which, when they become redundant, can be made into tables, garden pools, fountains, seats or flower-beds depending on their shape and the children's requirements. Obviously a lot of the features overlap so I just point them out in the form of notes.

*   *   *

A BALCONY GARDEN

Families who have flats or apartments can feel very frustrated for lack of fresh air and open space. But if you are lucky enough to have a balcony or flat roof next door, you will be amazed to see what you can do with it. In this confined area it is worth taking a lot of time and spending as much as you can afford to plan the best use of space. There should be room to sit and eat outside, then you must have pretty plants at all levels and, of course, you will want something to interest the children. The most important things to think of when planning a balcony are drainage and weight: roofs are not normally constructed to hold great weights, so choose light tiles or decking.

Notes
* Wood has been used throughout to give unity to the design.
* A built-in planting area dries out less easily than tubs, but must be well drained.
* Planting should include evergreen shrubs for all-year colour, plus bulbs and summer bedding.
* Climbers on the trellis and pergola might include a grape vine as grapes thrive in sheltered town settings. Children could grow sweet peas.
* A swing or seat can hang from the wooden pergola.
* The two small wooden planters are for individual children's gardens – perhaps herb gardens or miniature gardens.
* The sandpit has a wooden cover, offering extra sitting space.
* A built-in table is situated conveniently near the barbecue.
* A sundial on the wall.
* A bird-feeder hangs from the trellis.

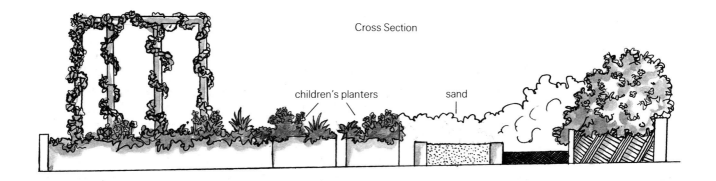

Cross Section

children's planters

sand

BALCONY GARDEN

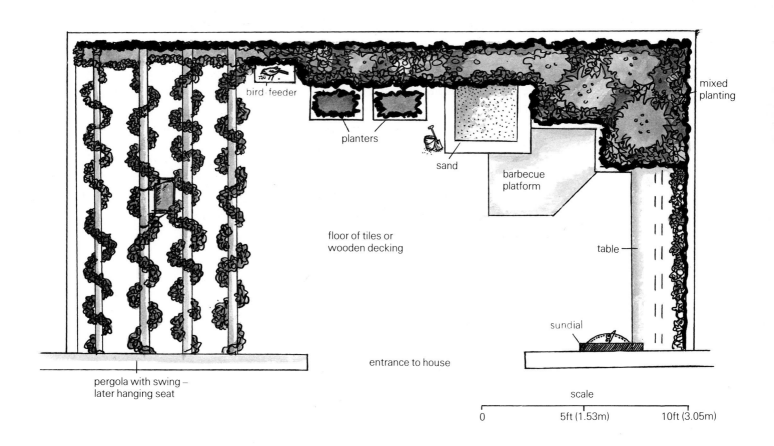

bird feeder

planters

sand

mixed planting

barbecue platform

floor of tiles or wooden decking

table

sundial

pergola with swing – later hanging seat

entrance to house

scale

0   5ft (1.53m)   10ft (3.05m)

A PATIO GARDEN

If your space is as limited as this, it would be impractical to dream of grass as it would get trampled in no time. In a small patio garden the materials you use are very important: they must wear well and look good, for it is very much an outdoor family room. Increase your seclusion and make a feature of the walls by building an attractive trellis and growing climbers like roses and vines.

In this garden we have allowed quite a lot of space for planting but kept it to the side. There should be a good basis of evergreen shrubs to give interesting colours all year round, but be sure to mix these with herbaceous plants carefully chosen for their flowers, stem colour, berries and so on as children love to observe the changing seasons through flowers. It is also very useful to grow pretty herbs like rosemary, sage, marjoram, mint and thyme.

Notes
* The central play area and surround is hard-wearing, attractive brick.
* The balustraded sunken sandpit has a built-in seat made of natural
  wood. It could later be a bog garden or a pool.
* The small tree could be an acer or prunus or a fruit tree like apple or
  pear.
* The bird-bath and bird-feeder are easily visible.
* Sculpture includes animals among the planting and a sundial on the wall
  above the sandpit.
* There is space for a small trough or tub gardens for children.

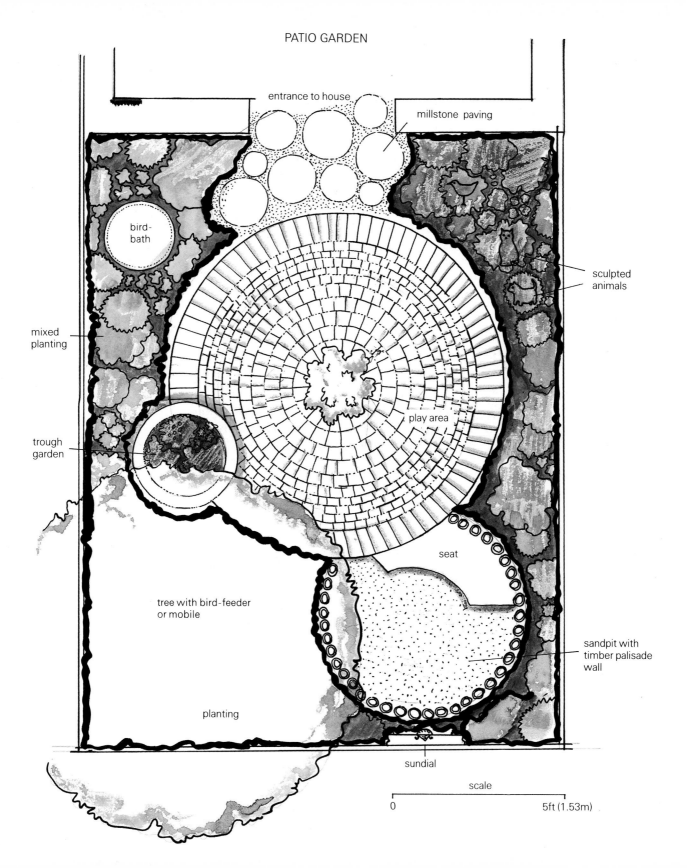

PATIO GARDEN

entrance to house

millstone paving

bird-bath

sculpted animals

mixed planting

trough garden

play area

seat

tree with bird-feeder or mobile

sandpit with timber palisade wall

planting

sundial

scale

0

5ft (1.53m)

A PAVED SMALL TOWN GARDEN

Even though there isn't a great deal of space, in this little garden we have attempted to create two separate areas. The different surfaces and the diagonal step help achieve this effect. A lawn is again out of the question. Interesting materials are essential and wood-decking or some attractive tiles are suggested for the upper area, but bear in mind that whatever it is will have a lot of wear. There is very little area available for planting and we have concentrated it in one clump easily visible from the house. However, there are high climbing plants on all the walls which should give a good general effect of greenery. They also provide happy homes for birds.

Notes
* The planting is mostly evergreen shrubs with herbaceous plants and annuals for summer.
* The pergola is for climbing plants and doubles as a swing.
* An octagonal sandpit has sides of brick or textured concrete and will later become a pond for water plants and fish.
* In the corner is a statue which would be particularly popular if it had moving parts.
* Tubs are for children's miniature gardens.
* The storage box below the pergola is for fold-up seats or toys and doubles as a seat.
* Birds are attracted by nesting-boxes and a bird-bath on the pergola.

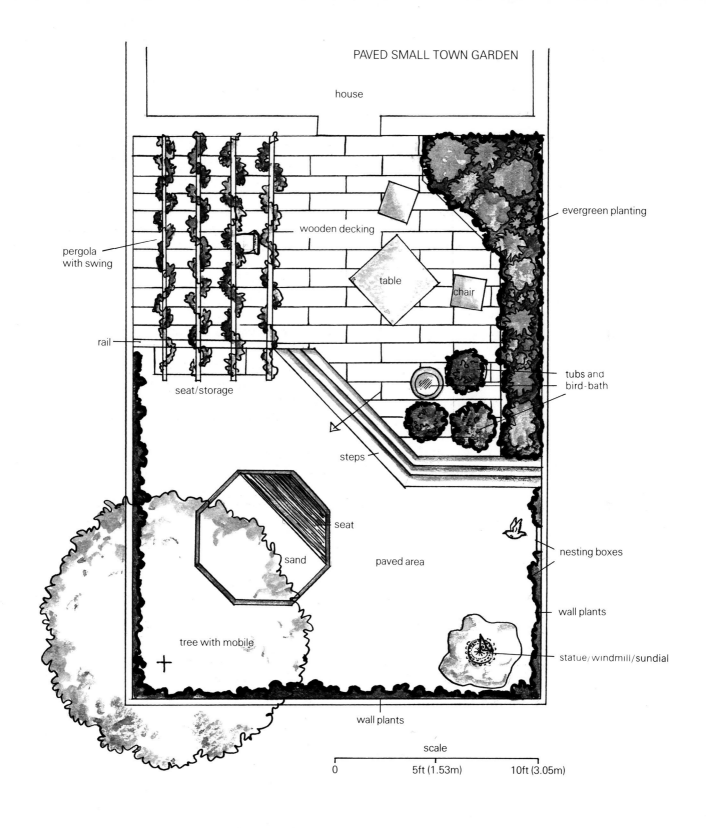

PAVED SMALL TOWN GARDEN

house

wooden decking

evergreen planting

pergola
with swing

table

chair

rail

tubs and
bird-bath

seat/storage

steps

seat

sand

paved area

nesting boxes

tree with mobile

wall plants

statue/windmill/sundial

wall plants

scale

0   5ft (1.53m)   10ft (3.05m)

A SMALL TOWN GARDEN

This garden is a bold concept involving a good deal of building and it would be expensive to construct, but the end result gives the children a lot of play area and the adults room to breathe. We have constructed a high playdeck which doubles as a sort of climbing frame with its ladder and slide. Below it there is useful storage space and also a wendy house with a soft play surface such as plastic grass. A pretty idea is the bubble fountain which has the advantage of being totally safe and of endless interest to small children. It also doubles as a bird-bath.

Notes
* Planting is raised to stop children accidentally messing.
* We suggest you plan the planting to attract birds and butterflies (see chapter 10).
* The timber terrace has room for permanent seating.
* The pergola can hold a swing, to be removed when not in use, and windchimes.
* Climbing plants cover the trellis and pergola for a lush effect.
* A small sandpit with lid doubles as a useful play table.
* The small tree might be a rowan or crab apple or an edible fruit tree.

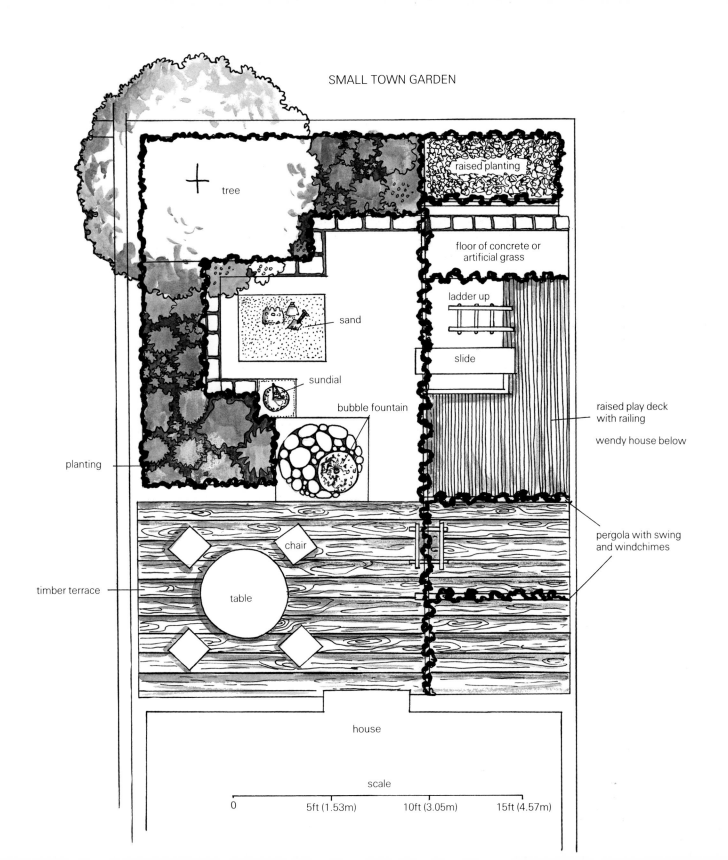

SMALL TOWN GARDEN

raised planting

tree

floor of concrete or
artificial grass

ladder up

sand

slide

sundial

bubble fountain

raised play deck
with railing

wendy house below

planting

pergola with swing
and windchimes

chair

timber terrace

table

house

scale

0   5ft (1.53m)   10ft (3.05m)   15ft (4.57m)

NEW HOUSE – SHORT-STAY GARDEN

Anyone who has ever moved into a newly built house knows just how depressing the garden can be. It is generally full of builders' rubble, has no grass and will soon be made into a mud patch by the children who will then transfer the mud into the house. In spite of this, most people foolishly ignore the garden and concentrate instead on the inside of the house. Only when that is finished do they start work on the garden – by which time they have quite often exhausted their supplies of energy and money. The really important rule is to plan the house and garden together.

The first thing to do when you move in is to clear out all the builders' rubble and lay turf all over. This immediately gives the children a play area and gives you time to breathe and plan. The squareness of the typical plot is very boring, so we have attempted to break it up with a sweeping lawn which still leaves lots of room to play.

Notes
* The large brick terrace leaves room for a portable sandpit and paddling pool plus table and chairs.
* There is room for swings, climbing frame etc. on the lawn.
* The small tree is chosen for blossom and berries – say a sorbus, apple or pear, or a prunus.
* Climbers like roses, honeysuckle and ivy will soon cover up the new fencing.
* The corner area round the sundial is the children's garden.
* The garden shed will hold tools, tables and chairs and a portable barbecue.
* The bird-bath can easily be seen from the house.
* A bird-feeder hangs on the tree and a bird-box on the fence.
* Tubs on the terrace are for herbs and miniature gardens.

NEW HOUSE – SHORT-STAY GARDEN

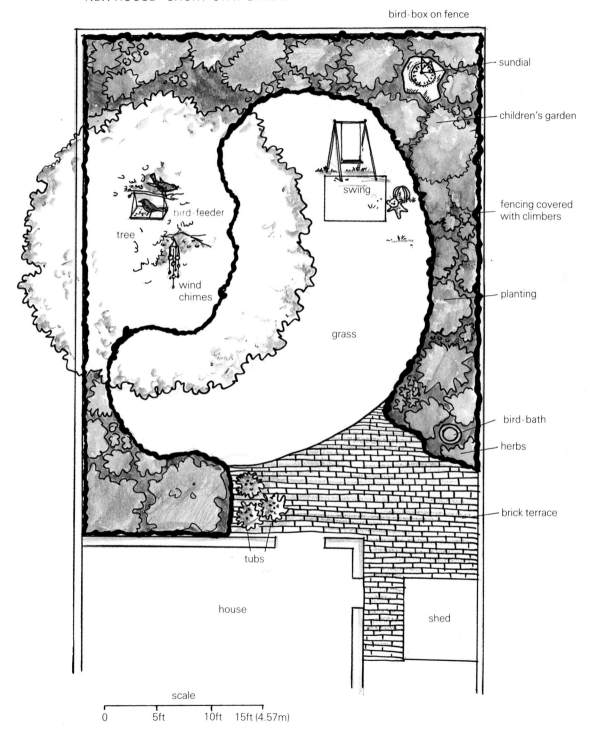

bird-box on fence

sundial

children's garden

fencing covered
with climbers

planting

bird-bath

herbs

brick terrace

swing

bird-feeder

tree

wind
chimes

grass

tubs

house

shed

scale

0   5ft   10ft   15ft (4.57m)

A LONG TOWN GARDEN

Because of the way many older town houses were built in terraces with rooms on three or four floors, most of their gardens are long but fairly narrow. At first sight they are not very appealing: they look like long, green tunnels, often with high walls on either side. But if carefully designed you can use this shape to advantage because it offers more scope for dividing the garden into rooms with different functions – the adult and toddler area leading to the proper garden, then a good play area with rough grass for games and a rather private section at the end. And if you have a narrow garden like this, you should make the most of your walls. Lots of climbing shrubs will provide good cover for birds.

Notes
* Room for children's individual garden plots, plus two miniature gardens on the terrace.
* A good area for slides, jungle jims and swings, and make the most of two existing trees to sling up a hammock.
* A sandpit on the terrace with a wooden lid.
* On the terrace wall, a fountain with a funny face.
* The terrace has a built-in barbecue.
* There are nesting-boxes on the walls and a bird-table on the terrace.
* A high trellis cuts off the last section of the garden containing the garden shed and compost bins. It also provides a secluded area for the wendy house which is built next to the shed.
* Space for a rabbit hutch.

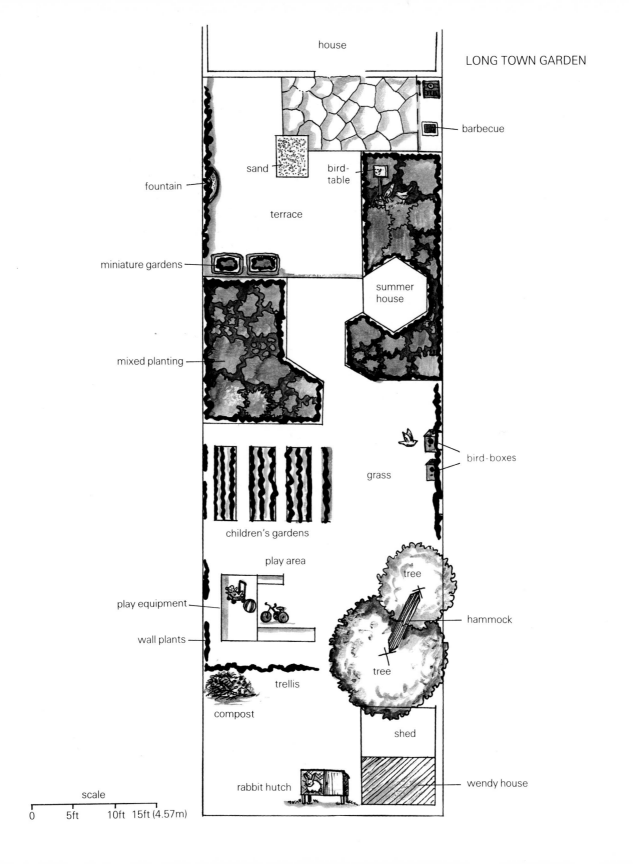

house

LONG TOWN GARDEN

barbecue

sand

bird-table

fountain

terrace

miniature gardens

summer house

mixed planting

bird-boxes

grass

children's gardens

play area

tree

play equipment

hammock

wall plants

tree

trellis

compost

shed

rabbit hutch

wendy house

scale
0   5ft   10ft 15ft (4.57m)

A SMALL SUBURBAN GARDEN

The larger your garden, the more uses you can get from it. This one is clearly an older garden with some well-established trees and an ideal wilder area which the children can use; firmly separated from the world of adults, they will certainly have more fun. So this is where we have put the swings and tree houses. It is also where bird- and bat-boxes should be hung, but distanced from the centre of activity. The grass should be kept quite long, so spring bulbs and summer wild flowers can bloom and animals and birds feel at home. You can even buy packets of wild flower seeds for such meadowy places. Another new feature is the ambitious earthworks in the central lawn. This forms a marvellous play area with a grass bank and sandpit and could later be developed to make a natural-shaped swimming pool or pond.

Notes
* There is plenty of space for herbaceous planting.
* There is room for a small vegetable garden safely fenced off along with a children's garden.
* Allow large shrubs to grow in the wild area as good dens for hide-and-seek. Also plant buddleia bushes which attract butterflies.
* Build a wendy house or have tents in the wild area. A rabbit hutch or perhaps a chicken shed might also be a good idea.
* The sandpit on the terrace later becomes an ornamental pool.

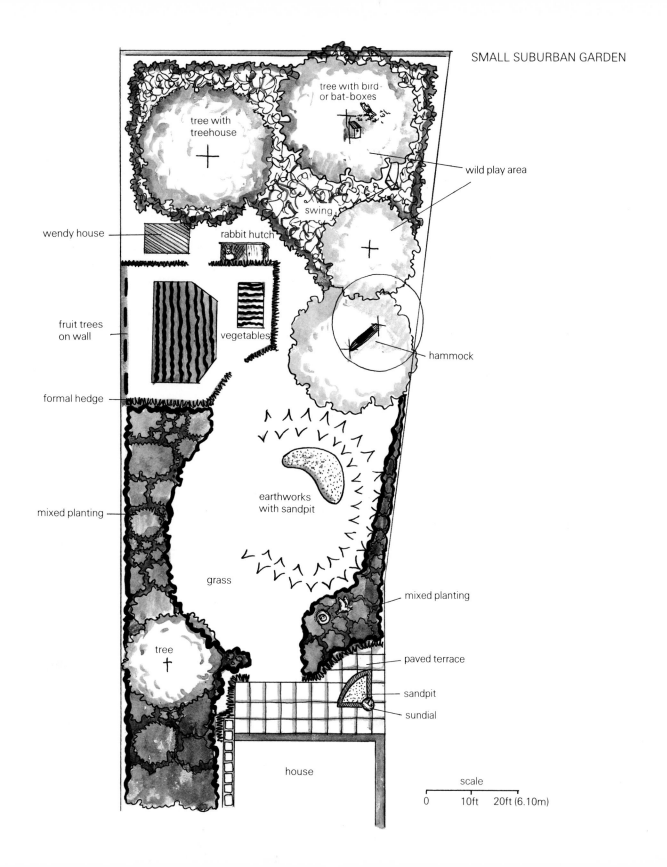

SMALL SUBURBAN GARDEN

tree with bird- or bat-boxes

tree with treehouse

wild play area

swing

wendy house

rabbit hutch

fruit trees on wall

vegetables

hammock

formal hedge

mixed planting

earthworks with sandpit

grass

mixed planting

paved terrace

tree

sandpit

sundial

house

scale

0   10ft   20ft (6.10m)

A LARGE FAMILY GARDEN

This large house and garden is for the family with several older children and so the garden must cater for all ages and tastes as well as providing vegetables and fruit to feed the family. You could set aside a substantial 'wild' area with copses of trees, including fruit trees, where there can be swings, tree houses, hammocks and nesting-boxes for birds – but remember to site the nesting-boxes away from the centre of play. If you take care to fence them off carefully, you might even have a beehive or two in this part of the garden and there would be space to keep a few chickens and geese. If you can afford it, build a tennis court – it would provide hours of fun and become the centre of a lively social life.

Notes
* There is a good-sized terrace at ground level and then a higher verandah under which there is room for a sandpit and toy and furniture storage.
* In the wild area allow for an earthworks where children can dig and build for themselves and make as much mess as they like.
* The wild area could contain a wildlife pond.
* There is a good-sized lawn for ball games but with some extensive planting around it.
* A high rose hedge separates the games area from the secret garden which contains swings, slides, jungle jims, a rabbit hutch and the wendy house.
* Around the wendy house there is ample space for a child's cottage garden decorated with statues and shells, with pebble paths and patches of annuals.
* A barbecue is stored under the verandah for use on summer evenings.
* The large vegetable garden is conveniently close to the house. Later it could be reduced in size to make more room for flowers or perhaps a swimming pool.
* Tools are kept in a shed under the verandah.

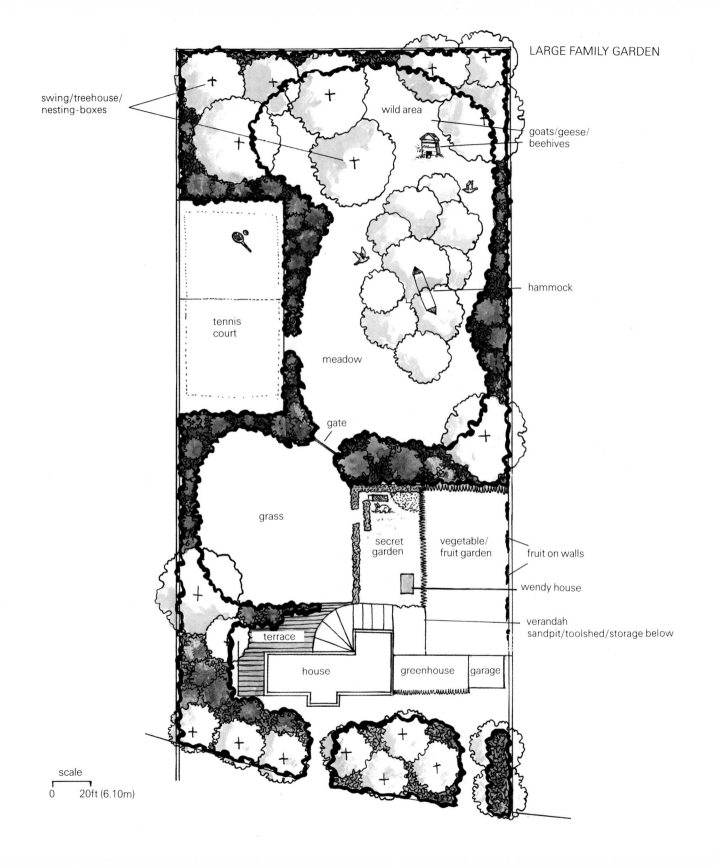

LARGE FAMILY GARDEN

swing/treehouse/nesting-boxes

wild area

goats/geese/beehives

hammock

tennis court

meadow

gate

grass

secret garden

vegetable/fruit garden

fruit on walls

wendy house

terrace

verandah
sandpit/toolshed/storage below

house

greenhouse

garage

scale

0   20ft (6.10m)

AN AMERICAN GARDEN

To me the ideal home stands back in its own grounds with a lot of space on all sides. This kind of suburban home is more common in America. The lack of fencing at the front means that children can freely mix with other children along the street and the fact that the house stands well back with a sidewalk and trees separating it from the road makes it comparatively safe.

The plan here assumes that there will be a lot of eating outside and we have designed a large terrace area with low walls for extra seating space. There is also a special barbecue area.

Notes
* Planting round the house is evergreen flowering or berried shrubs such as azaleas, scimmia, pieris and hollies.
* Plant flowering trees like cherries, magnolias and dogwoods, maples and Chinese elms for striking foliage.
* Plant bulbs in the longer grass around the house and round the shrubs. Many of these should be spring bulbs to flower as the cherries blossom, to be followed later by summer ones such as day lilies.
* The terrace is ideal for toddlers and there is a covered space for a sandpit and for storing outdoor play things and the paddling pool.
* On the terrace hangs a bird-feeder easily visible from the house and close to the kitchen.
* Because the overall plot is square the lawn is laid in two parts – a good round lawn for games and a lawn for climbing frames and a swing which could later be replaced by a swinging seat.
* The wide area of tarmac in front of the double garage is ideal for roller-skating safely away from any smaller children.
* There is a small area for growing salad vegetables and herbs. Children might have individual plots in the same place.

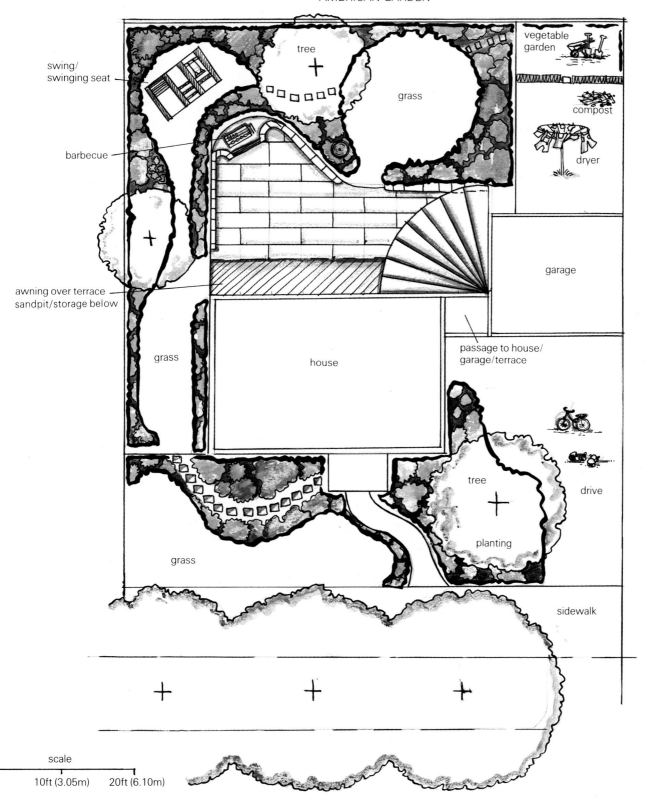

swing/
swinging seat

barbecue

awning over terrace
sandpit/storage below

vegetable
garden

compost

dryer

tree

grass

grass

grass

house

garage

passage to house/
garage/terrace

tree

planting

drive

grass

sidewalk

scale

0   10ft (3.05m)   20ft (6.10m)

A WILDLIFE GARDEN

Children naturally love wildlife and from about the age of six they can begin to take a really constructive interest. This is when you should start adapting the garden in consultation with them. Our design is not for a particularly large garden but should provide enormous scope for encouraging birds, animals and insects to venture in and take up residence. (See chapter 10 for more information about attracting wildlife into your garden.)

This garden has a good start because it has a natural stream running through it which is dammed at one point to form a shallow pond. This is where fish, frogs and newts, and insects like dragonflies and spiders can live and breed, and birds and animals feed and drink. The other very important feature of this garden is its hedge which gives infinitely more scope for wildlife than a wall or fence. It should be made up of a mixture of evergreen and deciduous shrubs and trees which provide invaluable shelter and food for birds and animals. When determining the make-up of the hedge, the important thing is to choose shrubs that are local. So in England a mixed hedge of hawthorn, holly, field maple, elder, dogwood, pyracantha and hazel would be ideal. Elsewhere just go for the native shrubs that birds are used to for this will attract them to nest and provide cover for the many animals and insects such as fieldmice and butterflies.

Notes
* There is very little formal planting. Choose plants like herbs which attract insects and butterflies.
* The central tree could be a fruit tree like a crab apple, apple or wild cherry which birds love.
* Sow wild flower seeds in the meadow area to provide seed for birds and nectar and pollen for bees and insects.
* After the dam the stream tumbles over log waterfalls.
* Over the stream you can build an attractive bridge.
* Near the house is a small pond in a trough for birds and plants.
* The summer house is good for bird-watching, close to the bird-table. It could be camouflaged by shrubs and perhaps a clump of hazel.

WILDLIFE GARDEN

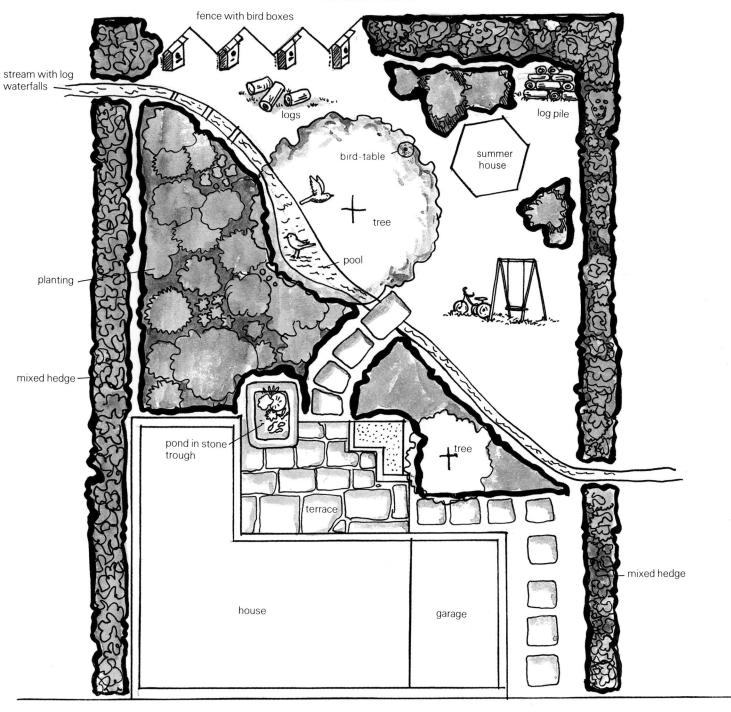

fence with bird boxes

stream with log waterfalls

logs

log pile

bird-table

summer house

tree

planting

pool

mixed hedge

pond in stone trough

tree

terrace

mixed hedge

house

garage

scale

0   10ft (3.05m)   15ft (4.57m)   20ft (6.10m)

road

A Garden for Children

* There is an area of special fencing for bird-boxes.
* You might put a bat-box in one of the trees.
* Dead logs will provide cover for mice and homes for toads and many of the insects which are the diet of birds such as wrens, robins and thrushes.

HOW DOES YOUR GARDEN GROW?

'And can all *flowers* talk?'
'As well as you *can*,' said the Tiger-lily. 'And a great
deal louder.'
'It isn't manners for us to begin, you know,' said the
Rose, 'and I really was wondering when you'd
speak!...'
'Aren't you sometimes frightened at being planted out
here, with nobody to take care of you?'
'There's the tree in the middle,' said the Rose. 'What else
is it good for?'

THROUGH THE LOOKING GLASS

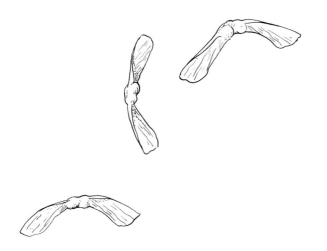

HOW DOES YOUR GARDEN GROW?

IT often surprises me how ignorant and incurious adult gardeners are about what makes their plants tick. It stands to reason that if you have a basic understanding of how plants grow, you will make a better gardener. Children, however, are nothing if not curious, so you should be well briefed.

Children say 'Why?' to everything. Why do you water flowers? Why don't flowers grow in the dark? What are the roots for? What is soil made of? and so on. To many of these questions the answers are extremely complex. But don't shirk. The older the child, the more he or she will grasp. Later in this chapter I shall describe a few experiments shown to me by a scientist who tried them out with his own children, with great success. Meanwhile here is a question and answer session which will, I hope, be of some help. Let's start with the soil because for a plant to grow and flourish, it must have good soil.

What is soil made of?
Soils vary enormously from place to place and this is largely due to the different proportions of ingredients. Soil is made up mostly of tiny particles of rock that have gradually been breaking down over thousands of years. If they are very fine like powder, then there is very little air between them and they make a very thick heavy soil. This is what clay soil is like. If, on the other hand, they are large, this makes a light sandy soil containing more air through which water can run more easily. Another important ingredient of soil is humus, a mix of the decomposed remains of organic matter such as leaves, roots, dead animals and insects that live in the soil. Soil also contains many chemicals on which the plants feed and water which

takes the chemicals up into the plants through their roots. Finally soil contains air which provides the necessary oxygen for the plants.

What does soil do?

A plant's roots are buried in the soil, so the soil acts as a kind of anchor to keep the flower or tree in place. It also acts as a reservoir for the water and contains the air and chemicals without which the plants would be unable to survive. Finally it provides a home for many insects and animals, some of which, like earthworms, are a great help as their constant movement airs the soil.

How do you improve your soil?

The ideal soil is what we call a good loam. If you pick up a handful of soil in a vegetable garden that has been well tilled for many years, you will find that it is both firm and crumbly, holds water well but is not sticky. This is because over the years gardeners have been improving the soil by adding things to it. You can do this too. The thing they have been adding most frequently is humus, probably in the form of manure or rotted garden compost. This breaks down to provide useful chemicals for the plants but also improves the texture of the soil while helping it hold a good balance of water.

How do you make humus?

Every good garden should have a compost heap. This is the easiest and most practical way of making humus because you are just re-using kitchen waste – rotted apples, lawnmowings, old vegetables etc. – in a practical way. Given time they will break down like magic to become pleasant-smelling compost. This you should put back into the soil in spring and autumn.

A compost bin should ideally be about 90cm (3ft) square and 90cm (3ft) high, made of wood, bricks or whatever is to hand. But it is important that the air can get in at all levels so that the compost does not turn sour, and the contents should be mixed loosely so that there is never too much of any one thing. In summer you can produce good compost in as little as twelve weeks because heat speeds up all chemical changes. In winter

it takes much longer. Remember that the heap should never dry out: add water if it looks like doing so.

Why do we add fertilisers?

Fertilisers are made up of chemicals which will help plants to grow and thrive. The three most important chemicals that a plant gets from the soil are nitrogen, potassium and phosphorus. In addition different plants like a little iron, sulphur, magnesium, calcium and cobalt which they get from a good soil.

Chemicals

Nitrogen is the chemical which helps plants grow, particularly their leaves and stalks. If plants are small and have yellowing leaves, the chances are they are short of nitrogen. Peas and beans cleverly pick up some nitrogen from the air, but most plants take it from the soil dissolved in water.

Phosphorus keeps a plant healthy, helping it to form good seeds and to build up resistance to disease. It also improves the root system, meaning that it is particularly important for root vegetables such as beetroots and radishes.

Potassium is vital for fruit crops, particularly tomatoes and soft fruit like strawberries and raspberries. It helps the berries to form and improves their flavour. It is also essential if flowers are to blossom well. So if you look at the list of contents of special rose fertilisers, you will find they contain a lot of potassium.

Lime is an ingredient which many soils contain and which helps green vegetables, fruit trees and many flowers to grow. But some plants, like heather and rhododendrons, cannot stand it and will not grow and blossom in limey soil.

Compost and manure are natural fertilisers but most of us cannot get enough for our garden's needs and so we add commercial fertilisers. There are two kinds of fertilisers: the first are organic, made from natural sources, and they tend to last longer in the soil. One of the best-known varieties is bonemeal which is literally made from crushed bones; it contains a high proportion of phosphorus and lasts a long time. Another natural fertiliser is dried blood which is particularly strong in nitrogen. And wood ash has for hundreds of years been used as a natural supply of potassium.

The man-made fertilisers usually contain a balanced combination of nitrogen, potassium and phosphorus. These dissolve quickly and are used up fast by the plants. Some fertilisers contain more nitrogen and are for leafy plants, others more potash for fruits and roses.

Grow two tomato plants side by side. Feed one regularly with a potash fertiliser and the other just with water and see the difference.

How do you find out what your soil needs?
By testing it – and you don't have to be a chemist to work out that if you have good soil you will grow good plants. It is easy to analyse your soil and it is fun to do, too. Buy a soil test kit which any older child will love to use. It will come with test tubes and special solutions with which to carry out four simple tests to help you establish first how acid or how alkaline your soil is (according to what is known by chemists as the pH scale), and then how much nitrogen, phosphorus and potassium it contains.

How do plants grow?
Plants need food (i.e., chemicals) to grow and these are dissolved in the water in the soil which is drawn up through the roots and then taken from the roots through the stems to the leaves by a process called vernalisation. Children will eventually learn about this at school. The green parts of plants can also make food by converting the sun's energy to starch in a chemical process called photosynthesis.

This means that all plants need some light and most of them need a lot of direct sunlight if they are to flourish. If a plant is deprived of light it cannot convert new energy to use and will eventually die. Over the centuries different plants have adapted to different conditions – those in tropical forests have grown used to moist shade, while those from deserts are accustomed to continuous sunlight – so not every plant needs the same amount of light. But if you take two identical plants (say sunflowers) and plant one in a sunny bed and the other in a dark corner that gets no sun, you will notice the difference in their growth.

Plants which are kept in dark or shady conditions will also grow very weak and straggly. A good way of demonstrating this is to put two plants side by side and cover one of them with a large plant pot with a stone on its head. Within a week you will see the change and know for sure that plants need light.

Why do we water plants?

It is an amazing fact that ninety per cent of a growing plant is water. It therefore stands to reason that, as it loses a lot of water by evaporation in the warm, it will need a new supply. Plants do most of their drinking at night. On a really hot day you may see them begin to wilt but they will look totally revived in the morning providing there is enough water in the soil.

What happens when soil is waterlogged?

Soil contains a lot of air which in turn contains oxygen which plants – like humans – need to live. If the water in the soil cannot drain away, then the plants are unable to take in the oxygen they need and will drown. This is why it is important that we dig the soil over and add sand and grit to improve the drainage.

When should you water plants?

Always water plants last thing in the afternoon or, failing that, first thing in the morning. This is because water will only get down to the roots if the top soil is wet and when the sun is shining the water will evaporate from the top very quickly. If you give a really good water in the cooler part of the day then the soil has time to soak it up allowing the plant to feed.

What do roots do?

As a plant grows its root system becomes much more elaborate and the original root (called the tap root) produces many smaller offshoots. These

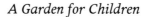

will both anchor the plant in the ground and provide a very efficient system for it to extract as much water and goodness from the soil as it needs. The roots of a mature tree spread as widely below ground level as the branches you see above.

How do plants increase?
There are a number of ways in which plants reproduce:

Seeds or spores
Most trees and plants reproduce from seeds which are embryo plants protected by a skin and containing reserves of food to help them start to grow. All trees and plants have flowers which produce seeds but reproduction only takes place when pollen is taken from one flower to another either by bees or other insects or by the wind. This explains why you may have a bad apple or bean crop when the weather has been wet and cold at blossom time: the insects have been sheltering rather than pollinating the flowers.

Once fertilised, plants produce seeds in seed pods after the flowers have died. When they are ready they spread in all kinds of clever ways: in fact, some seeds like the sycamore and the dandelion have special attachments which help the wind to blow them far from their parent trees. Seed pods like love-in-the-mist explode showering seeds over a wide area.

Some seeds are carried by animals or birds who eat them for their outer coating. Birds love berries and rely heavily on them for their winter food. But the stones inside the berries which contain the seed are often dropped or are eaten and then dispersed in the birds' droppings. This is one of nature's very practical ways of distributing seeds.

Once a seed is settled in favourable growing conditions and has sufficient water, it will start growing right away as long as the weather is warm enough. In chapter 12 I show how seeds can be grown indoors so you can watch the process at first hand, but first it is fun to analyse a seed. Leave a bean seed to soak overnight to enable you to remove the tough jacket which protects the inside: if you then cut the seed down the middle you will be able to make out the embryo which contains the start of a root and a shoot. The rest of the seed is made up of food for the embryo to feed on – just as the white of an egg provides nourishment for a growing chick.

58

Seeds put down roots first so they can take in water and absorb the nutrients which will enable them to produce the first tiny shoots of a new tree or flower.

Bulbs

Plants like daffodils and tulips grow from bulbs. While it is true that daffodils produce seeds, they reproduce most effectively when their bulbs grow smaller side bulbs which eventually divide off and become separate plants. A bulb contains all the food that the growing flower needs, though it puts out roots to get water. This is why you can grow a hyacinth bulb in a glass of water without either soil or chemicals. However, in this case it is unlikely that the bulb would flower again because it would have used up most of its goodness. Only by being in good soil can a bulb build up a new supply of food for the next year. Corms such as crocuses reproduce in the same way.

Runners

A fair number of plants put out baby plants on long runners which provide a source of nutrition from the parent plant until the offspring has been able to establish roots of its own. The runner then shrivels up. The best-known example of this form of propagation is the strawberry plant. I am particularly fond of indoor spider plants which grow lots of tiny plants on long runners which can be potted up separately and given to friends.

Division

Clumps of perennial plants can be carefully divided up and planted separately and will make new clumps again. It is actually good for big clumps of plants like phlox to be divided periodically. Iris rhizomes require division of a different kind: although they look like bulbs and corms, they do not produce new plants unless the rhizomes are cut or broken into sections and the old woody parts discarded.

Cuttings

Many plants and shrubs can easily be increased by taking cuttings: just take a youngish shoot of a growing plant and put it in earth, water it and wait for it to develop its own roots. To accelerate this process, you might add sand to the earth or special rooting powder to the stalk to encourage the plant to make roots. The easiest plants to take cuttings from are geraniums or pelargoniums. Many children will enjoy doing this particularly as these plants last all summer. (See Chapter 12 for more details.)

Grafting

Grafting is a man-made method of increasing plants, most commonly used with roses and fruit trees, and it involves sticking a branch of one kind of plant on to another that is closely related. The reasons for grafting are 1) that you can guarantee that the new plant will be exactly the same as the one from which the branch has been cut and 2) that often the prettiest roses and tastiest apples do not have good roots. Thus a good-looking rose is grafted on to a sturdy root (called a root stock) to get the best of both worlds. If you look at the base of most rose bushes, you will see a gnarled area – evidence of the grafting.

Why do some flowers last from year to year and some for only one summer?
Some flowers cannot stand frost and so die in the autumn. Others, known as 'hardy' can survive from year to year though they tend not to flower in the winter.

Flowers (not bulbs or corms) are generally divided into the following categories: hardy annuals, half-hardy annuals, hardy perennials and hardy biennials.

Hardy annuals are seeds like candytuft, cornflower and calendula which are sown outside in spring to flower that summer. In the autumn they die back and will not flower again the following year.

Half-hardy annuals are flowers like petunias and nicotiana (tobacco plant) which are sown in early spring to flower the same summer but cannot stand frost. In temperate climates like that of Britain and much of the United States they are started off indoors or in greenhouses and are then planted out in early summer when the last frosts have gone.

Hardy perennials will flower from year to year in the same place. These are flowers like Michaelmas daisies and achillea which are sown as seeds in summer. In the autumn the little plants are transferred to the place they will flower the following summer.

Hardy biennials are less common. These are plants such as forget-me-nots and wallflowers which only flower for one summer. However, unlike hardy annuals their seeds have to be sown a whole year before, so they are sown in summer in seed beds then planted out in the autumn in the beds where they are to flower the following spring or summer.

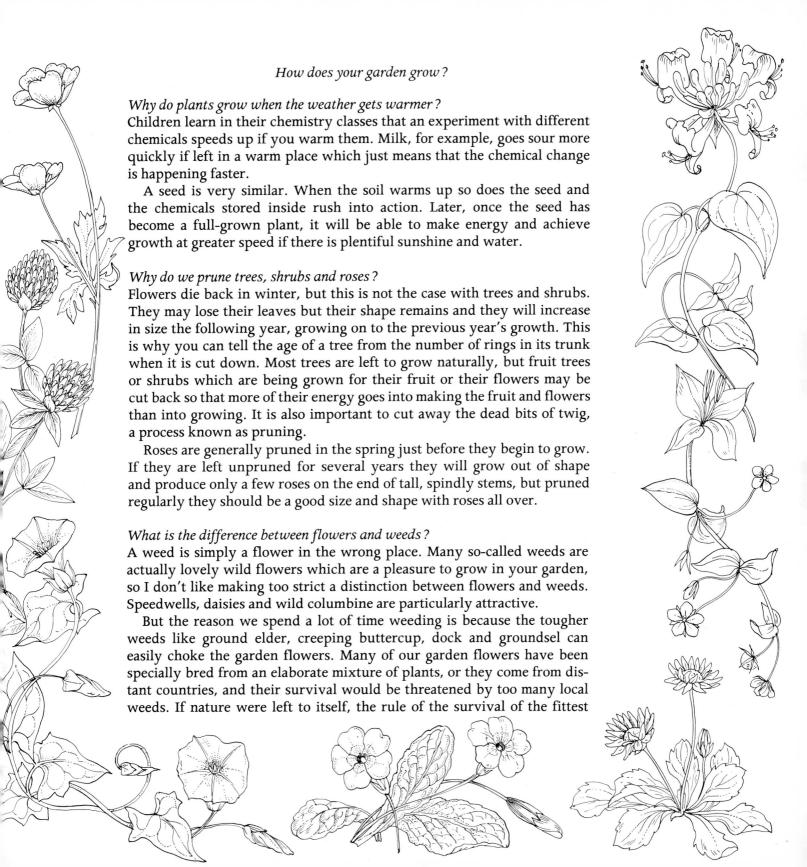

How does your garden grow?

Why do plants grow when the weather gets warmer?

Children learn in their chemistry classes that an experiment with different chemicals speeds up if you warm them. Milk, for example, goes sour more quickly if left in a warm place which just means that the chemical change is happening faster.

A seed is very similar. When the soil warms up so does the seed and the chemicals stored inside rush into action. Later, once the seed has become a full-grown plant, it will be able to make energy and achieve growth at greater speed if there is plentiful sunshine and water.

Why do we prune trees, shrubs and roses?

Flowers die back in winter, but this is not the case with trees and shrubs. They may lose their leaves but their shape remains and they will increase in size the following year, growing on to the previous year's growth. This is why you can tell the age of a tree from the number of rings in its trunk when it is cut down. Most trees are left to grow naturally, but fruit trees or shrubs which are being grown for their fruit or their flowers may be cut back so that more of their energy goes into making the fruit and flowers than into growing. It is also important to cut away the dead bits of twig, a process known as pruning.

Roses are generally pruned in the spring just before they begin to grow. If they are left unpruned for several years they will grow out of shape and produce only a few roses on the end of tall, spindly stems, but pruned regularly they should be a good size and shape with roses all over.

What is the difference between flowers and weeds?

A weed is simply a flower in the wrong place. Many so-called weeds are actually lovely wild flowers which are a pleasure to grow in your garden, so I don't like making too strict a distinction between flowers and weeds. Speedwells, daisies and wild columbine are particularly attractive.

But the reason we spend a lot of time weeding is because the tougher weeds like ground elder, creeping buttercup, dock and groundsel can easily choke the garden flowers. Many of our garden flowers have been specially bred from an elaborate mixture of plants, or they come from distant countries, and their survival would be threatened by too many local weeds. If nature were left to itself, the rule of the survival of the fittest would prevail and your garden flowers would be swamped by weeds, quickly returning to its naturally wild state. It is equally important to keep weeds out of your vegetable garden or very few decent vegetables will be produced.

Why do plants have such complicated names?
Learning the Latin names of plants is difficult, but I find older children are very interested once they realise that a plant's name often explains a great deal about it. From its name you might be able to discover where the plant first came from, who discovered it, what its leaves or flowers are like in shape and colour, or what time of year it appears. Of course it's a help if you know a bit of Latin but it is not essential because there are a number of useful dictionaries of plant names which can tell you a lot in detail.

For a start, the lovely davidia or handkerchief tree is named after the monk David who discovered it and forsythia after the plant hunter Forsyth. Japonica after a name (like *Camellia japonica*) indicates that a plant comes from Japan, *sinensis* means from China, *hispanica* from Spain, and so on. Or a name can describe the area a plant comes from: *Clematis montana* is clematis from the mountains, *alpina* means from the Alpine regions, *maritima* from the seashore and *sylvatica* from the woods. Other words describe the ways in which plants grow: *horizontalis* means spreading sideways, *pendula* means weeping, and *prostratus* means clinging to the ground or flat. *Vinca major* is a larger plant than *Vinca minor* and a *Rhododendron arboreum* would be treelike.

When describing leaves, *angustifolia* means narrow, *hirsutum* hairy, *latifolia* broad-leafed and *velutina* velvety. With flowers, *floribunda* means free-flowering, *macropetala* many petalled, *stellata* starry and *nutans* nodding. Then of course there are the colour descriptions. *Alba* is white, *purpura* is purple, *nigra* is black, *aurea* is golden, *argentea* is silver, *lutea* is yellow, *rubra* is red, and so on.

Names might also describe the scent of a plant. Thus *Viburnum fragrans* is a sweet-scented variety whereas *Viburnum foetidum* is unpleasant smelling and *Viburnum odoratissimum* is the sweetest scented of all. There isn't room here for a longer list, but this will give you a hint of the fun you can have deciphering plant names.

EXPERIMENTS

The following are experiments which a scientific friend of mine has carried out with his children aged nine and eleven, obviously with great enthusiasm from all the family.

Make a mini-greenhouse
To show how the warm conditions in a greenhouse speed up a plant's development, next spring just put a polythene bag over some twigs on the branch of a tree. You will see that the buds race ahead of those on the other branches. Alternatively, put jam jars over a few young seedlings in a row of seedlings, then watch as they develop much faster than their neighbours.

Demonstrate transpiration
One sunny day put a jam jar over a growing plant. In quite a short time you will find that the jam jar gets misted over as the plant transpires, letting water out of its leaves into the surrounding air.

Show how water grows up through plants
Pick a flower, preferably one with a rather translucent stem like a busy Lizzie, and stand it in a jam jar in a solution of water mixed with coloured ink. You will then be able to see the coloured ink growing up through the stem of the plant. If you do this with a white flower, say a carnation, and leave it overnight the colour will go up into the petals of the flower giving you a carnation with streaks of blue, red or green.

Make a fungal garden
Put a slice of moist bread in a polythene bag or in a bowl with cling film or cellophane paper over the top and leave it in a warm but shaded part of the kitchen for 7–10 days, examining it each day. You will notice that a fungus develops quickly, with quite dramatic changes of colour from red and blue to grey and black. It can look very beautiful and is even more interesting if you have a magnifying glass. After about a month the bread will disappear and the fungi will die.

Games with photosynthesis

Cut out the initials or the name of a friend in thick paper and then sellotape that paper over a growing leaf or a fruit such as an apple. Leave it for at least two weeks, then remove the paper and you will find the letters written there in bright green whereas the rest of the leaf or fruit will be pale by comparison. Pick it immediately and give it as a present to the friend, or press the leaf right away and make it into a bookmark or a card.

Find out about plant colours

The colours in a rose petal, an autumn leaf, soft fruit like elderberries or raspberries or roots like beetroot are made up of anthocyanins. These are soluble in water and the different colours that make up any one colour can be separated quite easily by a process called chromatography.

Get a piece of blotting paper and a jam jar with 1cm ($\frac{1}{2}$in) of water in the bottom. Mash up the petals, berries or leaves in a bowl with a few drops of water to make a coloured extract. Put a drop of this colour near the bottom of the sheet of blotting paper, then stand the blotting paper in the jam jar and leave it for a few hours. You will find that as the water moves up the blotting paper the soluble colours rise and are separated at different levels depending on the degree of their solubility in water. Incidentally, lots of anthocyanins are dependent on the pH in water, so if you add a little salt or vinegar to the water you will get a different range of colours.

Grow blue flax

You can grow blue flax from seed and it has pretty blue flowers on long stems. As these are used to make linen, you might attempt some weaving which is a lot of fun. Cut the stems and leave them to steep in water for a week. Then beat them and you will have flax fibres with which to weave something like a table mat. You can do the same with stinging nettles. There is a fairy story about a princess who had to weave special nettle coats for her brothers before they could be transformed from swans to people. But obviously nettles sting and you should put on thick gloves before you touch them.

Show how root systems work

Take a wooden seed or fruit box and remove one side. Substitute a plate of glass. Fill the box with compost and sow your seeds, taking care to sow some just next to the glass side. This will enable you to watch the root system developing through the glass.

Show how gravity works with seeds

Attach a broad bean seed to some blotting paper with a pin. Place the blotting paper in a jam jar with 2.5cm (1in) of water in the bottom and leave the bean, placed about halfway up, to grow. You will see that the root grows downwards and the shoot grows upwards. Then turn the bean upside down with the root pointing upwards. Within a few hours the root feeling the pull of gravity will begin to turn downwards and the shoots upwards and you will end up with a very wiggly-looking bean.

Show how good soil helps a plant

Take three small plant pots. Fill one with sand, another with garden soil and the third with good compost, then sow an identical plant seed in each one. Water them regularly and keep them all in the same conditions. The one sown in compost will make excellent progress, followed by the seed sown in soil, though the one sown in sand will be a poor specimen. You might then add some liquid fertiliser to the plant in sand and watch to see how it peps up.

See the benefits of an earthworm

Find two big jam jars. Put a layer of sand on the bottom of each and then a layer of peat, then sand, then peat again. Surround them both with black paper and put some dead leaves on the top. Add some earthworms to one. Within a short time you will see that they have mixed up the sand and peat and eaten the leaves.

Demonstrate the harmful effects of pests

Take two trays of seedlings. Into one of them introduce some bugs like leatherjackets, then wait to see how the plants develop. You will notice that the bugless tray progresses much faster and more evenly because the leatherjackets are eating at the roots of the other seedlings.

Find out why plants need light

Sow three pots full of cress seedlings. Place one in total darkness, another in all-round light and the third in a space where it only gets light from one side (i.e., a cardboard box with a hole in one end). You will quickly realise that light controls the growth of a plant because the one in total darkness will grow very tall and spindly, the one in even light will grow a regular shape and the one in the cardboard box will grow towards the light.

Make spore prints

Buy some flat mushrooms and chop off the stalks. Get a piece of paper and press one of the mushroom caps gently downwards. Leave it there overnight and you will find that it has left a print in spores. These will fall off if you move the paper but if you spray the print very gently with hair spray it will stick in place making a fascinating and pretty pattern. You will find that different fungi leave different spore prints, and you can do the same with ferns which also have spores on them.

Take a look at plant cells

With a simple microscope you can easily see plant cells. If you have privet berries in your garden squeeze some of them on to a glass slide and observe them. You can then do some simple experiments: show how osmosis works, for example. Water is taken into a plant by osmosis (i.e., it percolates through the porous skin) but the rate depends on the salt concentration. If you add some tap water to your crushed privet berries you will observe the cells (which contain salt) burst as they take in the water. However, if you add salted water you will see the cells shrivel up because the water is being taken out of the cells into the water which contains more salt than they do.

See how glycerine stops plants drying out

Take three parts water to one part glycerine and mix it in a jam jar. Then stand a flower or some leaves in it in a light, cool place and the glycerine will preserve the plant. This is very effective if you use beech leaves and makes it possible to have wonderful winter flower arrangements.

Experiments with agar

Agar is an extract of seaweed used a lot in cooking because it makes a transparent jelly. But it is also very good for growing things on – fungi, for example – and is used scientifically in experiments involving cloning. One interesting experiment is to make some agar on a flat plate, place the palm of your hand on it, then cover the plate with cellophane. You will see the germs from your hand grow. Another idea is to cut up a carrot into lots of pieces, place them on a plate of agar and cover with cellophane. Each piece will start an identical plant.

I never did experiments like these as a child. But I am sure that if I had done so the biology and chemistry classes at school would have proved altogether more interesting sessions and science would have become more relevant to my daily life.

STARTING TO GARDEN

'"Oh, thank you," I said; "I like gardening very much.
I should like to garden like you. I've a spade, and a hoe,
and a fork, and I had a rake, but it's lost. But I know
Papa will find me another; and I can tidy my own beds,
so the gardener need not touch them; and if there was
a wheelbarrow small enough for me to wheel, I could
take my weeds away myself, you know." . . .

Mr Andrewes kept up his interest in my garden.
Indeed, I soon got beyond the childish way of gardening;
I ceased to use my watering-pot recklessly, and to take
up my plants to see how they were getting on. I was
promoted from my little beds to some share of the large
flower-garden. My father was very fond of his flowers,
and greatly pleased to find me useful.

Some of the happiest hours I ever spent were those in
which I worked with him in "the big garden".'

A FLAT IRON FOR A FARTHING

STARTING TO GARDEN

NOW that I have explained the basics of how plants grow, the next step is to start putting all this knowledge into practice. Before children begin to garden they must have the right tools, for if they cannot do the job properly they will easily become disheartened. Miss Gertrude Jekyll, in her charming book *Children and Gardens* published in 1908, suggested that parents should arrange for the local blacksmith to make special small spades and trowels for children. This sounds a quaint idea today when there are not many blacksmiths to be found and those that have survived would probably charge a huge amount if you managed to track them down. But I notice that in lots of garden centres there are smaller tools which a child could happily use. Don't insult your children by giving them toy ones which will break.

Tools
The essentials are as follows:
1. A spade for digging, though obviously only larger children can use this by themselves.
2. A trowel for digging the flower-bed, planting out bulbs and for moving plants and weeds.
3. A fork for digging and weeding and breaking up the soil.
4. A hoe for weeding between the flowers and breaking up the surface of the soil.
5. A rake for levelling the soil, clearing surface stones and raking dead leaves. This can also be used as a useful measure.
6. A watering can with a fine spray for watering plants gently.
7. A small wheelbarrow with which to trundle implements around and in which to put weeds. These are very popular.

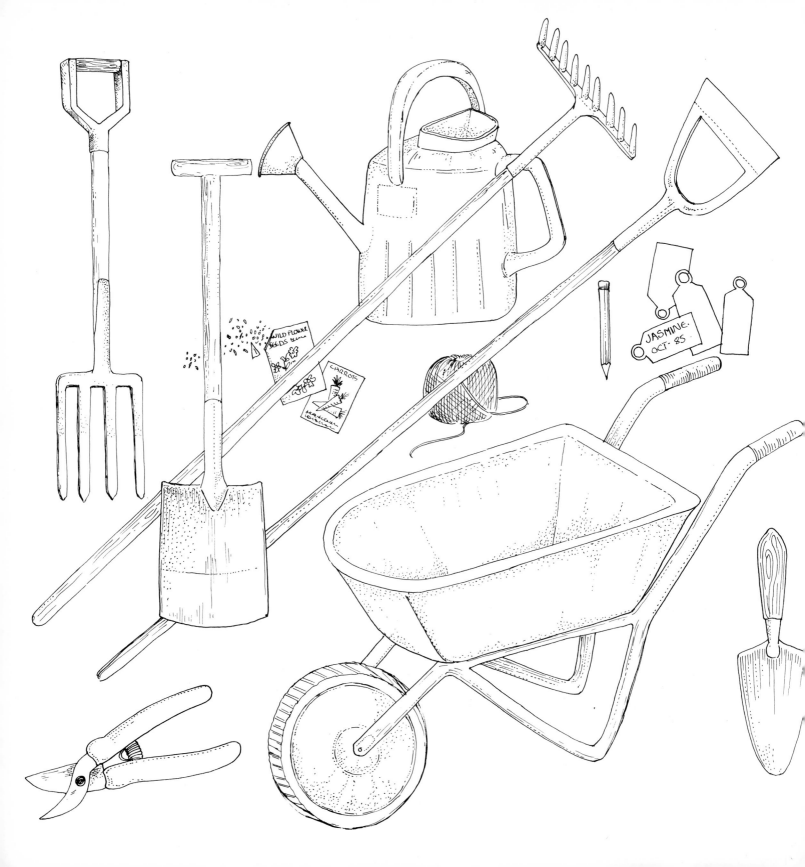

8. Secateurs for cutting and pruning plants and shrubs.
9. Labels and a marking pencil.

Clothes

If there's to be any serious gardening, it's important that children should be properly dressed: they need good rubber boots and warm clothes that you don't mind them getting dirty. When I was a child, we had special dungarees for gardening. They were rarely washed and became so caked in earth that they could almost stand up on their own. But it didn't matter and we felt totally happy in them.

Planning

First you must decide where the children's garden should be. If your overall space is small then you might only be able to set aside a tiny patch or a tub or trough. But if space is no problem, a flower-bed of, say, 2 × 1 metres (6 × 3 feet) would be fun. Older children might go as large as 3 × 2 metres (10 × 6 feet). The space should be big enough to provide a challenge but not so large that the weeding would make a child lose heart.

Every gardener needs an encouraging start, so be sure to select a good, sunny position to give the flowers every chance of flourishing. Most varieties of flowers benefit from direct sunshine. And see that the bed is quite near the house and a tap of some kind – carrying heavy cans of water is tiring and dispiriting work. If you are lucky enough to have a wendy house, then you might map out the garden in front of that.

The ideal time to start preparing a garden is in the autumn before the frosts begin. Most of it will simply be dug and then left over the winter months, but because you want to do some planting now it's important that at this point you have a plan of how the garden will be (in chapter 6 I talk about garden plans). Take some time over the planning stage using graph paper or lined paper marked to scale, pencils, a rubber and a ruler. It is an entertaining and totally engrossing evening job.

Smaller gardens should be kept narrow so that children can reach into the centre without having to tread on the bed. In the case of a large plot, lay a little path across it using small stepping stones. Children love grass and would certainly welcome the idea of having a little lawn in their garden, but it really is too dangerous for a child to mow so I would advise

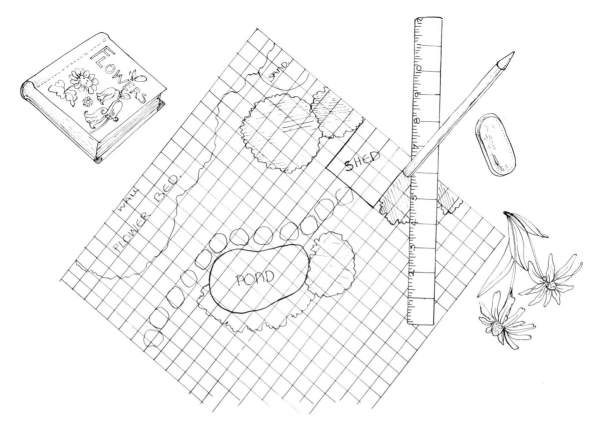

against it. If they are not to be deterred, make it a tiny one that can be cut by an adult with shears. Miss Jekyll's first garden — part of a large Edwardian garden — was long and thin with a path down the middle, so very easy to tend, particularly as she did it with her sister. I think sharing should be encouraged but it very much depends on the children in question . . .

Digging

Heavy digging is a hard job even for grown men, so help children with the digging of their plot in autumn and then again in spring. After that they should mostly be able to get by with a trowel and a hand fork. Once the area has been well dug for the first time, pull out all the big weeds and then leave the patch alone so that the winter frosts can break it up to make an ideal soil for sowing in the spring. At this point add compost or rotted manure to give the soil a more crumbly texture and make it more fertile.

Bulbs

In some part of the plot the soil should be firmed down, for autumn is the time to plant the bulbs which will bloom the following spring – you'll find a list of suggestions at the end of this chapter. Generally speaking bulbs should be planted at a depth of about twice their length. Add some long-lasting fertiliser like bonemeal to start them off well and water the bulbs immediately after planting.

Remember to plant bulbs in little clumps of at least three and probably more so they look natural but leave enough space for them to increase: try tossing them on the ground and planting them where they land so that they look as if they have sprung up naturally. But don't plant them where you hope to sow seeds in spring as they will be in the way. Plant them round the edge of your bed, perhaps, or along your path. Above all, remember to put a label indicating where they are or you could easily split one while digging.

Be sure to plant snowdrops because they will be the first to appear – sometimes when the snow is still on the ground – and are a very cheering sight at the end of winter. After they have bloomed remember to divide them up and they will increase much more rapidly. As the plot is probably not very large, I don't advise planting huge bulbs like lilies or the larger varieties of daffodils. Go for the smaller ones like scillas, chionodoxa, crocuses, little narcissi, muscari, *Anemone blanda*, little *Iris reticulata* and tulips like my favourite bright yellow *Tulipa tarda*.

Shrubs and roses

Shrubs and roses may be planted at any time during the winter when the ground is not frosted or waterlogged. I am not suggesting that roses are ideal for children's gardens because they can get too large and also, once they have been planted, there is nothing very interesting to do other than just to prune them once a year. However, they are an essential part of any secret garden and I shall return to them in Chapter 7.

It may be an idea to add a small evergreen shrub or tree just to give interest and introduce a contrasting shape. This would make a good Christmas present. Dig a large hole at least 45cm (18in) across and 45cm (18in) deep, allowing room for the roots to spread. Having put the shrub or tree

in place, fill up the hole with earth adding some compost and long-lasting fertiliser to encourage early growth.

Growing flowers from seed

In early spring the plot should be given another good dig and a weed, taking care not to disturb any bulbs or the roots of the shrubs that have been planted. Then it should be trodden over so the ground is firm. The first seeds may now be sown. A seed packet will contain many more seeds than are needed, so children may go halves with their friends. The best way to start sowing seeds outdoors is to do it in straight rows using a string attached to two pegs for guidance. This may sound unexciting but it is the only way to tell the difference between the precious seedlings and the weeds. Once the seedlings are larger they can be moved into other shapes or patterns.

Some seed companies sell special children's collections containing the seeds of a number of hardy annual flowers that are easy to grow, but you can find other ideas in my list at the end of this chapter. Even the smallest child can enjoy growing a sunflower: the seeds are large enough to be easy to handle and then it grows to a height of up to eight feet producing a flower like a blazing sun to amaze and thrill everyone.

I used to grow lots of nasturtiums when I was six and I still do: they have large seeds which are easy to sow and they produce vivid orange, yellow or red flowers. As an extra advantage, the leaves taste good in salads. Other personal favourites are orange calendula, pink and white candytuft, soft, blue nigella or love-in-a-mist, blue cornflowers and sweet peas which require stakes or a wall for support. It is marvellous to have sweet peas in the garden if you enjoy flower arranging because the more you pick them, the more they grow. I also love poppies, which after the first year, will seed themselves all over the garden.

If you want the plants to be ready to flower early, they should be sown indoors in boxes (as I show in Chapter 12), transplanted to pots when they are seedlings and finally put out in early summer. Do the same for the half-hardy annuals such as petunias, nicotiana, French and African marigolds, antirrhinum, impatiens and the marvellous helichrysum or everlasting flower which you can dry to look lovely in winter. In early summer lots of the half-hardy annuals are sold as small bedding plants in shops

76

and markets and can be bought for planting out immediately. This is more expensive and less exciting than growing flowers from seed, but it is definitely better than nothing. For late summer colour, I recommend asters.

The seed packets will say how deeply and how wide apart the seeds should be sown. Add some fertiliser to give them a good start, water after sowing and keep doing so regularly if it does not rain hard. Finally label each row of seeds or you will easily forget what is what.

Sowing vegetables and herbs

Children love growing vegetables, particularly the easy ones like lettuces and radishes or little tomato plants — ask for the bush varieties which can live outdoors and don't need stakes to hold them upright. But I know several children who have had great success with squash, pumpkins (which then become the Jack o'Lantern at Halloween) and marrows, and also with herbs. Home-grown vegetables and herbs, prettily packaged, make lovely presents.

Thyme, savory, marjoram and sorrel are easy to grow and are so useful in the kitchen that they are worth trying. They also smell good. Remember that mint will spread by its roots all over the garden, so grow it in a tub. Parsley, on the other hand, takes a long time to appear, so the soil should be kept moist.

If there is room it is great fun to grow runner beans up a wigwam-shaped frame made of tall stakes which then becomes an entertaining bean house. Start the beans off in little yogurt pots with earth indoors (again, see Chapter 12). These will germinate fast in a warm, light place and the light will be even more important as the leaves begin to show. Plant them out in early summer when the frosts have gone.

In a regular vegetable garden it is essential to rotate the crops, meaning that they should not be grown in the same place each year. The reason for this is that different vegetables take different chemicals out of the soil. Some of them leave good things behind — beans, for instance, leave nitrogen in the soil and so should be followed by vegetables like sprouts or cabbages that need it — but most crops give nothing back in return for the good things that they take and so the soil must be given time to replace them. In addition some crops leave diseases behind : cabbages leave cabbage club root, for example, so should not be allowed to hang around in the same

patch of ground. A rotation plan will help to ensure that no vegetables are in the same place two years running, though ideally there should be a three-year cycle.

Work in the garden

Once the seeds have been sown and watered keep an eye out for the little seedlings, but also look out for weeds – if they are not removed right away, they will throttle the plants and stop them growing. Weed the ground when it is wet so that the roots do not get left behind to start again and use a hoe or a fork and your hands.

Once the flower and vegetable seedlings are an inch or so tall they should be thinned out to the distance indicated on the seed packet. Always water well before transplanting so that fewer roots get broken and some of the earth attached to the roots is transferred at the same time. Have a well-watered place prepared to move them to at once. If there are spare seedlings they can be planted in old yogurt pots filled with earth and given to friends.

When summer arrives the flowers will bloom at last and that is the most exciting time of all. But a gardener can never sit back : the weeds are always close at hand and it will be necessary to keep weeding all summer if the plants are to flourish. It will also be important to water if it does not rain. Some flowers, like nigella and cornflowers, may need stakes for support. I always think that natural stakes made from tree branches look best, but otherwise you can buy bamboo or wood stakes. Tie the plants loosely to the stake with garden string.

Mulching

One marvellous way of keeping the weeds back and keeping moisture in the soil is by mulching. This means putting a layer of something over the soil to keep the weeds smothered and prevent the moisture in the soil from evaporating. A mulch is usually made of lawn cuttings, wood shavings or perhaps leaf mould. Some modern gardeners use black polythene, but this is very ugly and I don't recommend it.

Seeds

Most flowers will bloom better if they are not allowed to produce seed pods, so when a flower dies, off with its head before it has a chance to

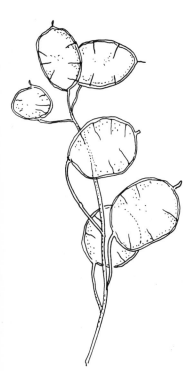

waste energy making seeds. Of course, towards the end of the summer you might keep a few seed pods to grow yourself the following year, although as many garden flower varieties are hybrids (a mixture bred from different varieties – like a mongrel) their children won't always look the same as the original flowers. But it's fun and cheap to do with, say, antirrhinum or love-in-a-mist, both of which have interesting-looking seed pods.

Pests

Flowers are frequently attacked by pests. Slugs and snails are a particular nuisance and are best deterred by ordinary cooking salt laid round your plants. They hate this and it kills them. There are also all kinds of effective insect sprays, but I am very loath to use them because they can kill the bees and butterflies at the same time and are dangerous if there are toddlers around. What's more, they are very expensive. Blackfly and greenfly will be killed if you spray them with soapy water, though not as efficiently as they would be by some of the chemicals. And there are various other traditional remedies such as planting marigolds near the vegetables to keep the aphids at bay.

Birds

Birds can also be a nuisance. There is nothing they like more than juicy young lettuce shoots. Of course, you don't want to hurt the birds, just keep them away from the plants, so the best plan is to attach bits of silver foil and brightly coloured paper and thread them along a piece of string. Tie each end of the string to a thick stick about two foot long. Plunge one stick firmly in the ground at one end of the row of lettuces so that about 18 inches shows above ground, then put the other stick at the other end with the string stretched tightly between them. The bits of paper will rattle and glitter in the breeze and, with luck, frighten the birds away.

The traditional bird-scarer is a scarecrow shaped to look like a man wearing a tattered hat and jacket. In my childhood we often used to see them standing out in the fields looking like lonely old men. Nowadays they seem out of fashion, but they are great fun for children to make and can be quite effective at keeping away large birds like pigeons which are an absolute menace among the lettuces. Other very entertaining and effective bird-scarers are windmills. They come in all shapes and sizes and children simply love them. They are often seen on English allotments.

Putting the garden to bed

By autumn, the garden will begin to look a bit bedraggled and it is time to pull up the annual plants and put the garden to bed for the winter. Throw the old plants on the compost heap and dig the bare bed over, adding compost to fortify the soil for next year. There is something very satisfying about the look of a well-dug garden, all neat and weedless.

A few winter flowering plants will provide a bit of colour in the bleakest months, particularly in areas where the snow will not be around for too long. I have already mentioned snowdrops. You might also think of planting heathers. These come in many colours from white to pink but the commonest ones are purple. Some have pretty coloured foliage which is interesting all year round, but many of them flower in winter as well.

The last thing to do in autumn is plant out some plants to flower in late spring or early summer; the wallflowers and forget-me-nots which have been grown in cottage gardens for generations. I really love the gay colours of wallflowers which fill a gap between the merry spring bulbs and the bright summer bedding and their other advantage is that they are nice and evergreen. Buy the low-growing compact varieties which also flourish in tubs and your garden will show an exciting promise of summer throughout the grey winter months.

FLOWERS FOR YOUR GARDEN

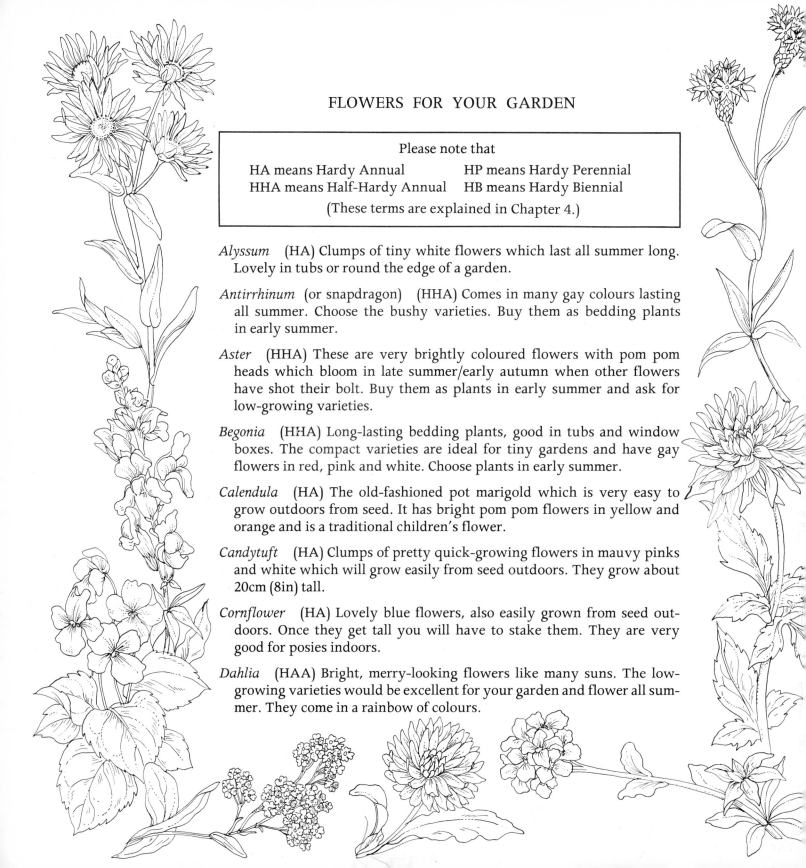

> Please note that
>
> HA means Hardy Annual   HP means Hardy Perennial
>
> HHA means Half-Hardy Annual   HB means Hardy Biennial
>
> (These terms are explained in Chapter 4.)

Alyssum   (HA) Clumps of tiny white flowers which last all summer long. Lovely in tubs or round the edge of a garden.

Antirrhinum (or snapdragon)   (HHA) Comes in many gay colours lasting all summer. Choose the bushy varieties. Buy them as bedding plants in early summer.

Aster   (HHA) These are very brightly coloured flowers with pom pom heads which bloom in late summer/early autumn when other flowers have shot their bolt. Buy them as plants in early summer and ask for low-growing varieties.

Begonia   (HHA) Long-lasting bedding plants, good in tubs and window boxes. The compact varieties are ideal for tiny gardens and have gay flowers in red, pink and white. Choose plants in early summer.

Calendula   (HA) The old-fashioned pot marigold which is very easy to grow outdoors from seed. It has bright pom pom flowers in yellow and orange and is a traditional children's flower.

Candytuft   (HA) Clumps of pretty quick-growing flowers in mauvy pinks and white which will grow easily from seed outdoors. They grow about 20cm (8in) tall.

Cornflower   (HA) Lovely blue flowers, also easily grown from seed outdoors. Once they get tall you will have to stake them. They are very good for posies indoors.

Dahlia   (HAA) Bright, merry-looking flowers like many suns. The low-growing varieties would be excellent for your garden and flower all summer. They come in a rainbow of colours.

Digitalis (or foxglove)　(HP) These romantic country flowers which appear in the Peter Rabbit books and so many other stories are very popular with bees. Buy plants in spring and put them at the back of your plot so they don't drown other plants.

Gypsophila (or baby's breath)　(HA) These hundreds of tiny white flowers on their stems seem to float in the air. Grow them from seed outdoors and cut them to make posies with other flowers.

Helichrysum　(HHA) The famous everlasting flower which you can buy as plants in early summer and then cut to dry when they bloom. Hang them in bunches indoors in a cool, dark place.

Impatiens (or busy Lizzie) (HHA) This is often grown as a pot plant indoors but it will be happy outdoors in summer when the frosts have gone. There are many colours and the little flowers bloom all summer.

Limnanthes (or poached egg plant)　(HA) Very bright low-growing buttercup yellow flowers with a white tip to their petals. They look like an egg sunny side up.

Lobelia (HHA) Tufts of tiny low-growing bright blue flowers which last all summer. Buy as plants in early summer and they will last till the autumn. They are also wonderful in tubs and window boxes.

Marigolds　(HHA) French and African marigolds sizzle with brightness. They come in vivid yellows and oranges and last all summer. Buy them as plants in early summer.

Mesembryanthemum　(HHA) Lovely clumps of pink, white, orange or yellow flowers with an interestingly shaped flower. Buy plants in early summer.

Myosotis (or forget-me-not)　(HB) A wonderful blue spring flower which you plant out in autumn and which flowers alongside the tulip bulbs.

Nasturtium　(HA) These are almost the easiest flowers to grow from seed outdoors. What's more they don't mind a poor dry soil. Their bright orange, yellow and red flowers look very gay in tubs.

Nigella (HA) Pretty love-in-a-mist grows outdoors from seed. Traditionally this is a bright blue flower whose strangely shaped seed pods you can see right away. There are also pink and white varieties.

Nicotiana (HHA) These sweet-smelling tobacco plants are becoming very popular. They come in bright but soft colours and last all summer. Ask for low-growing varieties which don't need stakes.

Pansy (HP) These merry-looking flowers really look as if they have faces. They are wonderful to grow as they go on all summer and last for years and years. Buy plants in autumn or spring and plant them on the edge of your patch so they don't disturb your spring-sown seeds.

Petunia (HHA) These are lovely summer bedding plants which you buy as plants in early summer. Their flowers are like French horns with crinkly edges and they bloom in many colours all summer long. They are very happy in tubs.

Poppy (HA) Poppies are such fun to grow. You sow them outdoors in spring and once they start to flower you will have difficulty getting rid of them. They make interesting-looking seed pods which throw seeds everywhere in the garden so new plants appear in unexpected places.

Primrose (HP) The traditional primrose is a soft yellow and blooms in spring. Now there are many other colours and if you buy a couple of plants in the autumn you may well be surprised. They will also last for years to come.

Rudbeckia (HA) Has large daisy flowers in brilliant yellow, orange or gold and lasts most of the summer.

Stocks (HHA) These come in soft whites, pinks and mauves and consist of tall clusters of flowers on an upright stem. Buy low-growing varieties as plants in spring. They smell lovely.

Sunflower (HA) This is the most famous children's flower because even the smallest child can sow it and enjoy the huge plant that appears like magic, growing to a height of about 2.5m (8ft).

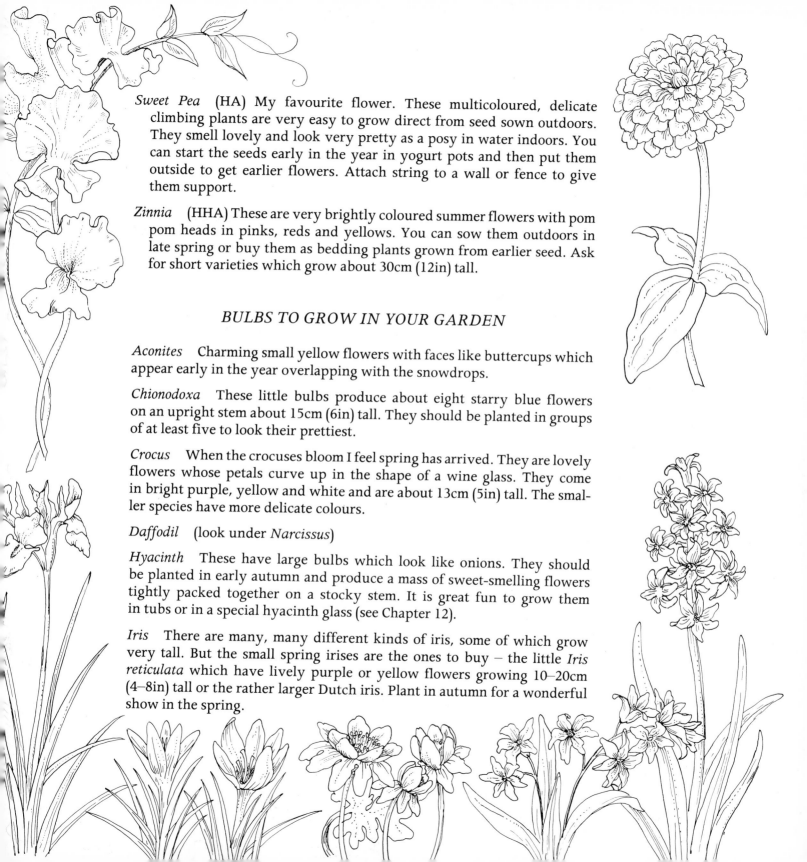

Sweet Pea (HA) My favourite flower. These multicoloured, delicate climbing plants are very easy to grow direct from seed sown outdoors. They smell lovely and look very pretty as a posy in water indoors. You can start the seeds early in the year in yogurt pots and then put them outside to get earlier flowers. Attach string to a wall or fence to give them support.

Zinnia (HHA) These are very brightly coloured summer flowers with pom pom heads in pinks, reds and yellows. You can sow them outdoors in late spring or buy them as bedding plants grown from earlier seed. Ask for short varieties which grow about 30cm (12in) tall.

BULBS TO GROW IN YOUR GARDEN

Aconites Charming small yellow flowers with faces like buttercups which appear early in the year overlapping with the snowdrops.

Chionodoxa These little bulbs produce about eight starry blue flowers on an upright stem about 15cm (6in) tall. They should be planted in groups of at least five to look their prettiest.

Crocus When the crocuses bloom I feel spring has arrived. They are lovely flowers whose petals curve up in the shape of a wine glass. They come in bright purple, yellow and white and are about 13cm (5in) tall. The smaller species have more delicate colours.

Daffodil (look under *Narcissus*)

Hyacinth These have large bulbs which look like onions. They should be planted in early autumn and produce a mass of sweet-smelling flowers tightly packed together on a stocky stem. It is great fun to grow them in tubs or in a special hyacinth glass (see Chapter 12).

Iris There are many, many different kinds of iris, some of which grow very tall. But the small spring irises are the ones to buy – the little *Iris reticulata* which have lively purple or yellow flowers growing 10–20cm (4–8in) tall or the rather larger Dutch iris. Plant in autumn for a wonderful show in the spring.

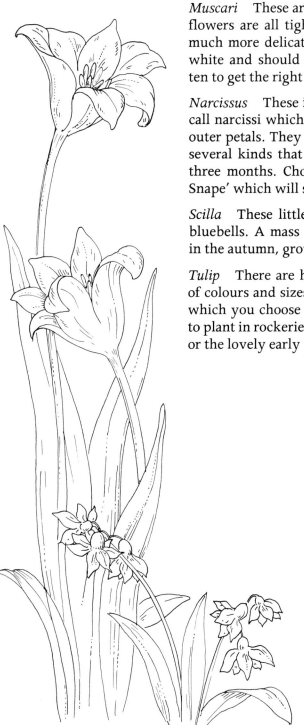

Muscari   These are often called grape hyacinth as their tiny grape-shaped flowers are all tightly packed like a hyacinth. But they are smaller and much more delicate, just right for a small garden. They come in blue or white and should be planted in autumn in clumps of between five and ten to get the right effect.

Narcissus   These include daffodils with their long trumpets and what we call narcissi which have short trumpets, often a different colour from the outer petals. They are such cheerful yellow or white spring flowers. Plant several kinds that flower at different times and they will last for about three months. Choose the smaller varieties like 'Peeping Tom' or 'Jack Snape' which will suit a smaller garden and are anyway much prettier.

Scilla   These little spring flowers are generally blue and look like tiny bluebells. A mass of them in early spring looks simply delightful. Plant in the autumn, growing at least ten together.

Tulip   There are hundreds of different kinds of tulips in a huge variety of colours and sizes – from 8cm (3in) to over 60cm (2ft) tall. So, be careful which you choose for a small plot. The shorter ones which are often sold to plant in rockeries are ideal. Try bright yellow *Tulipa tarda, Tulipa greigii* or the lovely early *Tulipa kaufmanniana*.

A GARDEN OF YOUR OWN

'Great was my pride and delight when I was first
given a garden of my own, to do just what I liked with.
It was a long-shaped strip of ground notched out of the
far end of the shrubberies of the big home garden,
between them and a rising hedge-bank.'

CHILDREN AND GARDENS

A GARDEN OF YOUR OWN

NOTHING is more exciting for children than to see the seeds they have planted themselves first appearing, then growing and producing flowers. But it is especially exciting if those flowers are in their own gardens. I remember the thrill myself, just as Miss Jekyll did, even though she was writing as an old lady. And adults are just the same: they take much more interest in a garden if it is their own. I reckon that from about the age of six, children can have a thrilling time in their own gardens, although they will obviously need quite a bit of help from adults at the start and continual support and encouragement as time goes on.

We all like to be in charge of our own projects so children should be given the opportunity to design their own gardens and I guarantee they will be much more imaginative than anything their parents might dream up. First of all they should peg out their space and measure it, then take a sheet of paper – preferably graph paper because that will make it easier to draw to scale – and draw the garden plan using, say, 2.5cm (1in) to equal 30cm (1ft).

The added advantage of designing the garden plan on paper is that it is bound to stimulate the imagination, invite all sorts of merry possibilities. It might be great fun to choose a theme for the garden, for example: make a space-age garden or a prehistoric garden, or take ideas from books or nursery rhymes. Bring in props such as model animals, gnomes and fairies, bridges, bird-tables and bird-baths, wishing wells, little houses and stiles, all of which will add variety.

I have suggested six possible gardens, but obviously the choices are endless and these ideas are intended simply as stepping-off points for children's imagination. I have used a variety of shapes and plants to suit each theme – herbs in the Magician's garden, wild flowers in the Wild Things garden, bell-shaped flowers for 'Mary, Mary', vegetables for Peter Rabbit, and so on. In many cases I have packed far too many things in for a small garden, so my suggestions should definitely not be followed slavishly.

Nearly all children, when asked to design a garden, will include water. This is fairly impractical and can lead to very muddy scenes: however, you might make a small pond by lining a hole with thick polythene, though only if there are no toddlers about. Alternatively you could make a make-believe river out of paving-stones or gravel and use it as a path.

AN ALICE IN WONDERLAND GARDEN

We know from Lewis Carroll's book that Alice looked through the door and found 'the loveliest garden you ever saw'. It was full of bright flowers, so that gives us a start. But I am sure that any child reading *Alice in Wonderland* will come up with lots of ideas about what to include.

My plan would feature a giant ornamental mushroom just like the one upon which the Caterpillar sat. You'll find one in most garden shops. And a table for the Mad Hatter's tea party should also be central as children could then have picnics in their garden.

Then there could be something to represent the wood in which Alice meets Tweedledum and Tweedledee – a shrubby corner with evergreens like laurel could be planted at the back, for example. Fear of the Queen of Hearts forced the frantic playing cards to paint the white roses red and so in my drawing I have suggested red and white roses. Obvious white roses to choose would be 'Iceberg' or 'Pascali' which bloom all summer long, or perhaps tiny 'Little White Pet'. A good crimson one is 'Lili Marlene'. But roses are expensive and prickly so perhaps some red and white bedding plants like alyssum, petunias, antirrhinums or impatiens would do just as well.

The cards provide the excuse for a formal bedding scheme which so many children love. First peg out the shapes of hearts, diamonds, clubs and spades. Make a white background of low-growing alyssum. Dark blue or mauve flowers would substitute for black clubs and spades: try lobelia,

ageratum or purple alyssum. Good small reds would be little begonias or impatiens. Plant the flowers closely, say 15cm (6in) apart to produce a mat-like effect.

The area around the table is where the prettiest mixture of plants might grow. So far our colour scheme is red, white and blue, so this can be broken up with splashes of yellow, orange and pink to produce an exciting colour combination. In spring there should be small daffodils, tulips, scillas, crocuses and muscari which will stay in the ground from year to year. Come summer the bedding plants take over with candytuft, asters, zinnias, calendula and brightly coloured marigolds. This mixture will provide you with a thrilling colour scheme all summer long.

MR McGREGOR'S GARDEN

'First he ate some lettuces and some French beans; and then, feeling rather sick, he went to look for some parsley.

But round the end of the cucumber frame, whom should he meet but Mr McGregor.'

No child today can avoid knowing about Peter Rabbit and so I think a Mr McGregor garden would be a very popular idea. This, of course, would be a kitchen garden designed entirely for vegetables. We can find in the stories the names of a lot of the vegetables that Mr McGregor grew, but you need not stick to them exactly and in fact some things like gooseberry bushes would be most unsuitable, being prickly and far too large. Cabbages should also be excluded as they take a long time to grow and most children don't like eating them. However, there's still a good selection of small, tasty vegetables which any child would enjoy growing, particularly as they will give quick results. One huge marrow or pumpkin plant could be especially exciting.

The garden should ideally be square or rectangular, like an old-fashioned kitchen garden. And it should be fenced, if possible, to keep the Peter Rabbits out and also to enable you to grow thornless blackberries and

loganberries. Once you have dug over the plot and raked it, I suggest that you lay out vertical and horizontal paths with stones or just packed earth, crossing in the middle to make four beds. In one of these put a scarecrow dressed in an old tattered coat (preferably blue as that was Peter Rabbit's colour), a scarf and hat.

A small part of the garden should be a seed bed where lettuce and herb seedlings can be started off before being transplanted to the main area to replace those that have already contributed to family meals. The gardener should have a lined exercise book containing the ground plan and a record of when, what and where things were sown and harvested. Be sure the seed is sown in neat rows so you can distinguish the vegetables from the weeds, and keep the seed packets after sowing and stick them into the exercise book. If you stick down the tops of the packets only, you will be able to remember the varieties and look up the instructions.

My suggestions for vegetables include radishes which come up very fast, herbs like thyme, marjoram and chives, carrots, lettuces (small ones like 'Little Gem' and 'Tom Thumb'), spring onions and perhaps runner beans up poles at the back. All these are easy to grow. Parsley is often difficult to begin with, but keep trying as once it takes it will grow in profusion. Later on, you might buy some small bush tomato plants.

The important thing is to see that this garden is weeded and watered regularly or the vegetables will not be worth eating. Some children might lose interest fast, but try and keep them at it as the results from this small space will be worth waiting for and the source of endless pleasure. If the plot is given a dose of manure in autumn or early spring, there will be no need to add artificial fertilisers.

Lastly, why not buy an ornamental rabbit for the next birthday?

A WIND IN THE WILLOWS GARDEN

'Never in his life had he seen a river before – this sleek, sinuous, full-bodied animal, chasing and chuckling, gripping things with a gurgle and leaving them with a laugh, to fling itself on fresh playmates that shook themselves free, and were caught and held again. All was a-shake and a-shiver – glints and gleams and sparkles, rustle and swirl, chatter and bubble. The Mole was bewitched, entranced, fascinated.'

This garden would centre on the river around which Kenneth Grahame's story revolves. The path could represent the river and along it would be the homes of Rat, Otter and, of course, Toad. Badger's house was in the Wild Wood and this offers an opportunity for planting shrubs and tall flowers to create an undergrowth. Mole lived in Mole End and we know that his house had a collection of statues outside which gives a lot of scope for garden ornaments. Toad Hall, on the other hand, was very grand, with splendid gardens, so that part of the garden could be quite formal while the rest should be very natural. In the centre there should be a picnic area beside the river: children will remember Mole and Rat's famous picnic and might want to have picnics there themselves.

When you have worked out the plan, dig the area over so it is ready for planting. Then stamp down the 'river' path and lay either stones, gravel or old slate. There may not be room to represent the island, but you might try, and don't forget to lay stepping stones to the Wild Wood and Toad Hall. On a river bank there would be bullrushes and reeds. Instead you might try ornamental ferns and grasses, but choose varieties which don't grow too tall. Concentrate them round the homes of Otter and Rat to provide good cover. In spring small yellow irises would look like water irises.

Toad Hall stood proudly with its lawns reaching down to the river. Try a more formal bed of edging plants like alyssum and lobelia with perhaps some bright French marigolds or small red begonias. The bright, rather vulgar colours would be just right for Toad. As the world's greatest boaster I'm sure he grew the largest flowers, so this is just the place for at least one huge sunflower. In spring Toad Hall could have small daffodils and tulips in the parks along with other bulbs.

Give a dark look to the Wild Wood by planting evergreen shrubs like laurel or *Viburnum tinus*, both of which have pretty white flowers. Avoid prickly hollies and mahonias. Against the wall plant a climbing thornless blackberry which should be a success. Rat, being a well-organised person, may have grown herbs and a few vegetables around his home, so you might plant parsley, lettuce, radishes and chives which you could eat in the picnic area.

Mole is my favourite character and while he was not that good at house-keeping – we first meet him making a mess of his spring cleaning – I'm sure he would have grown something. Pansies are the most winning-looking flowers so try them, and also plant lots of little wild strawberries – again for the picnics. Around the picnic area grow things that smell good : some tobacco plants and lavender would be lovely, and perhaps some antir-rhinums as well. Nasturtiums, which you could easily grow from seed, could look good and as an added bonus their leaves taste delicious in sandwiches.

THE MAGICIAN'S GARDEN

Herbs fascinate children. They smell rather interesting, they attract lots of bees and butterflies and you can eat them too. Through the centuries they have been used as remedies for illness and many of them still are today.

As the Magician spends a lot of time brewing up magic potions, it is clear that he would need lots of herbs. So his garden should be laid out in the traditional knot garden pattern used in herb gardens with little paths encircling small symmetrical beds. I have suggested a straightforward cross shape with a circle in the centre for a tub or a statue, or maybe a privet bush clipped to look like the Magician's cat. But it could be much more complicated than this.

Before you lay out the paths, dig the whole plot over adding good compost or manure and rake it evenly. Peg out the shape using sticks and string, then lay the paths down using pebbles, stones or slates. Traditional knot gardens have low hedges, often of box, round each bed. A pretty

fast-growing substitute is silver cotton lavender (Santolina) or you could use herbs like thyme, marjoram or parsley with the taller herbs behind.

Most herbs can easily be grown from seed, though in the case of angelica, lovage, fennel and rue it is hardly practical as you only need one or two plants of each. Lavender and sage are best taken as cuttings or bought as young plants. Mint should be kept in a tub to prevent it from spreading, but it is worth growing a number of varieties – such as apple mint, pineapple mint and spearmint – as they are such fun to smell.

In spring sow thyme, rocket, marjoram, summer savory, tarragon, parsley and sorrel. Do remember that plants should be labelled, particularly in this garden where there are so many types. It is terribly important that children remember to water the seeds regularly in the first weeks after sowing so they do not dry out. Also, keep weeding to allow them room to grow.

In late spring buy plants of angelica, fennel, rosemary, sage in varying colours of gold, red and green, rue and lovage. Feverfew, lavender and tansy are not much used for cooking, but they smell interesting and produce pretty flowers for the bees. In addition you can make lavender bags to give as presents.

Herbs in general make good presents. If the garden really gets going the children can dry them and store them in bottles to use in winter or they might even sell them to a local shop. There are many lovely herb books available and it's worth buying one to find the full range of things you can do with the produce from your garden.

A WILD THINGS GARDEN

'That very night in Max's room a forest grew and grew – and grew until his ceiling hung with vines and the walls became the world all around.'

Where the Wild Things Are is a book most children know and like. As it features forests which are very weird and wonderful, we would try to include some strange-shaped and exotic-looking plants in this garden. It would also be a true wild flower garden where many of the weeds less welcome in the rest of the garden, such as white trumpeted bindweed, buttercup and celandine, could find a home.

Designing a garden to look wild and natural is every bit as difficult as designing a formal one. Growing up the fence there might be dense climbers like our native ivy and blackberry bushes. Then plant some plants with unusual leaves like rhubarb or spiky ones like cordyline or yucca. Another rather exotic shrub is *Fastia japonica* with its glossy evergreen leaves and strange flowers, better known as an indoor plant. In the centre make a pool for Max's boat as instructed in Chapter 10. Soon it will be teeming with life.

Dig and rake over the rest of the plot. (Do not add manure or fertiliser to a wildlife garden because the flowers don't want such a rich soil.) Then the search for wild flowers begins. It is important to have a wild flower book so children know what they are planting and can identify a plant from its leaf as well as its flower. Always water a plant well some time before transplanting and take some soil attached to its roots. Tell the neighbours what you are up to and they may have wild flowers to contribute.

Never transplant flowers from the countryside. In any case in most countries this is illegal. Happily you can now buy many wild flower seeds and some nurseries are even selling them in pots. Those easy to grow from seed are ox-eye daisy, toadflax, scabious, heartsease, columbine, harebells, foxgloves and valerian. And there are many more. Primroses and cowslips are a little more difficult but the packet will generally give you the best advice. In the case of some of the commoner plants you won't need to buy packets, however: you can remove seed pods when they are ready. Then there are bulbs that grow wild like bluebells and species of daffodils.

Finally you might take cuttings of local climbers like the wild clematis (old man's beard), ivy and shrubs such as hawthorn which would all thrive in this setting.

Your lawn will probably yield pimpernels, birdsfoot trefoil, clover, buttercups and daisies. Avoid very common weeds like dandelions which would take over quickly and seed all over the rest of the garden. If the wild garden blooms well it should attract lots of insects including bees and butterflies. Keep notes of the plants that are introduced and their progress and the different insects and animals they attract.

A NURSERY RHYME GARDEN

Because nursery rhymes are traditional things, I feel that this garden should concentrate on old-fashioned cottage garden flowers. There are so many children's songs and rhymes to choose from and they vary according to country, but there are many areas of overlap. The ones I have chosen here come from my own childhood and I sing them with my children. You can include your own favourites, but try to find rhymes that go well with gardens.

The garden I have mapped out has a ring-o'-roses round a wishing well. It has Mary, Mary, Quite Contrary's garden including cockle shells. It has a low wall for Humpty Dumpty, a little nut tree on which you could hang the nutmeg and a pear, a bird-table for the four and twenty blackbirds and, most important, a teddy bear's picnic area where children can picnic too.

The big structural element in this garden is Humpty Dumpty's wall. Ideally it should be made of bricks or local stone or blocks and measure about 38cm (15in) tall and 30cm (12in) wide, making a good place for children to sit. They can also grow tiny rock plants in the crevices between the stones (in the case of bricks leave little gaps for the plants).

Rock plants are dazzling jewels, many of which come from alpine areas. Some are expensive but some, like mauve aubrietia, white candytuft, arabis and the many star-like saxifrages, will spread well and you can easily take cuttings from friends.

The rest of the garden should be dug over in autumn and good compost added. Then the roses should be planted, unless you decide to wait until very early spring. Choose floribunda roses which will not grow too tall but will flower all summer: brilliant yellow 'Allgold', crimson 'Rob Roy', orange 'Stargazer', 'Pink Parfait' and white 'Margaret Merril'. This might also be a good opportunity for a selection of miniature roses or that enchanting rose with flowers like a pink miniature, 'The Fairy'.

The paths could be laid out as stepping stones to help you find your way around this cottage garden. The picnic area could be grass kept short by an adult with shears. Build a really attractive bird-table up which you could grow climbing sweet peas and make the wishing well a shallow bird-bath.

In Mary's border go for bell-like flowers such as foxgloves, Canterbury bells and all kinds of campanula in shades of blue and white. Other cottage garden plants which children adore are huge hollyhocks – if you buy one plant it will seed itself over the years – and of course sunflowers. And further old-fashioned suggestions would include love-in-a-mist, cornflowers (though they will need staking), candytuft, poppies, calendula, nasturtiums and gypsophila, all of which can be grown from seed.

In spring the border could be a mass of bell-like spring flowers such as scillas, snowdrops, bluebells and the drooping-headed *Narcissus cyclamineus*. Use shells collected on holiday to decorate.

SOME CHILDREN'S GARDENS

'The children's gardens are very amusing. The four of them . . . Aileen's garden was dull but tidy and fairly full. Sylvia's garden was rather wayward, Barbara's absolutely neglected, Aubrey's garden, aged 4, is really wonderful, he watches things grow, knows the names of all his plants and is thrilled and thrilling over it, so wise and sensible, picks off dead things, weeds, waters, propagates with sense and care. He has a row of sweet peas and roared with laughter at the idea of their climbing sticks, he put them in under protest, now in transports of delight, they climb!'

LETTER FROM EDWIN LUTYENS TO HIS WIFE

MY KINGDOM

Down by a shining water well
I found a very little dell,
No higher than my head.
The heather and the gorse about
In summer bloom were coming out,
Some yellow and some red.

I called the little pool a sea.
The little hills were big to me.
For I am very small.
I made a boat, I made a town,
I searched the caverns up and down,
And named them one and all.

And all about was mine, I said,
The little sparrows overhead,
The little minnows too.
This was the world and I was king;
For me the bees came by to sing,
For me the swallows flew.

I played there were no deeper seas,
Nor any wider plains than these,
Nor other kings than me.
At last I heard my mother call
Out from the house at evenfall,
To call me home to tea.

And I must rise and leave my dell,
And leave my dimpled water well,
And leave my heather blooms.
Alas! and as my home I neared,
How very big my nurse appeared,
How great and cool the rooms!

Robert Louis Stevenson

SOME CHILDREN'S GARDENS

TRACKING down children's gardens is no easy task. It's as if they wanted to keep them a special secret. In my search for original ideas, I have looked at gardens created at school but these have tended to be less exciting than those at home. Of course, only a few of the gardens I have discovered are interesting and different enough to warrant inclusion – one row of sweet peas looks much like another – but here are descriptions of a handful developed by mostly local children which I thought were all particularly imaginative.

SUZY'S GARDEN

Suzy is nine years old and has been keeping a garden of her own since she was five. Her first garden was very small and she sowed it with the contents of a pre-mixed packet of fast-growing annual seeds, so what came up was a surprise. She says these packets are 'good for little children because they love the colourful mixture. But older children want to be able to make special patterns with flowers.'

Then her family moved to a garden that needed a lot of work. She was given a small plot on which she grew a few spring flowers like snowdrops and bluebells and in the summer she went in for edible produce, growing a fine line in strawberries and peppers. These strawberries were particularly successful and she had fun growing the runners into pots and selling the new plants in aid of charity in the street outside her front door.

Then she progressed to a larger plot. At first it was full of weeds so her initial efforts were rather hampered by bindweed but things are improving now. The garden is in a good sunny position and at about

4.5m × 1m (15ft × 3ft 6in) it is quite large. It has a fence to the left and slopes down to the garden path. On the right there is another path separating it from her younger sister's garden.

'I don't think any garden should be without water in it,' she says. Last year she installed a small garden pond as an experiment and was fascinated to see how many insects set up home there: her interest in natural history has been stimulated by attending weekend camps run by the children's conservation group Watch. This year she and her father are going to make a pond in another part of the garden and plan to build a rustic hut nearby from which to observe the wildlife.

Last year Suzy grew a mixture of seeds in rows. The most successful were love-in-a-mist (nigella) and candytuft. Cornflowers grew well but proved too tall, dwarfing everything else, and the calendula tended to wilt. But the really great excitement was the hundredweight pumpkin which grew so large it measured at least 75cm (2ft 6in). 'It took ages to hollow it out' but eventually it made a marvellous Jack o'Lantern for Halloween.

This year she is much bolder and has actually mapped out an ambitious plan for her garden involving a lawn and flower-beds and centring the scheme on a pond. On the two fenced sides she is planting that starry white-flowered shrub *Spiraea arguta*. In the pond there are two varieties of water lily – pink nymphaea 'Paul Hariot' and yellow nymphaea 'Sunrise'. Among the pebbles round the pond there are purple crocuses, then in wider circles further back she has planted annual flowers starting with low-growing candytuft, then dwarf larkspur, then nigella, then rudbeckia and finally tall larkspur on the outside circle. Around the bed she insists on growing grass because she loves the soft feel of new-sown grass and wants a little lawn on which to entertain her friends. It will, she says, be a very secret place. And the problem of mowing has been solved: 'I'll pay Dad 10p an hour to do it . . .'

A stepping stone path connects the garden path with the pond and along the side of the garden path there's a pattern of purple pansies and white alyssum. This plan is a considerable advance on last year's conception and bodes very well for Suzy's future as a gardener.

TOBY'S GARDEN

Toby is eight and has been gardening since he was six. He does most of his gardening in the spring and summer holidays and at weekends because during the week he is at school in town. He has a good-sized garden 4.5m × 3m (15ft × 10ft) which is part of the old raspberry patch of an old country garden.

His first horticultural efforts were in his parents' vegetable garden where he grew some delicious carrots and sweetcorn and had a go at growing a pumpkin – but with no success. Then two years ago he was given his own garden which his father dug over for him. But there was still the problem of the residual weeds which are always bad in the first year and so his sweetcorn and pumpkins have yet to flourish.

Last year, however, things began to come very right. His mother did the digging over and they got rid of a lot of the weeds before they started. They concentrated on making a more interesting shape and got some stones from the side of the road to make a path. Toby sowed radishes, carrots and some herbs and grew mint in a tub. But his great success came from concentrating on different kinds of squash. He grew cucumbers, which he raised as seedlings for a project at school, and also courgettes. His only problem was that he forgot to label them so could not remember which was which until they began to fruit.

Then there were a number of wonderful glossy ornamental gourds which grew to a good size in marvellous shades of bright yellow and green. He varnished them and gave them away as table decorations for Christmas. And the crowning glory were the pumpkins – five of them, the two largest being very heavy indeed. One was used in church at Harvest Festival and another was hollowed out as a lantern for Halloween.

This year Toby is going in for squash again and plans to grow a giant marrow to enter in the local village show. He has also dried seeds from last year's tomatoes and planted them in fibre pots at school. Last year his mother said that every weekend, the minute he arrived home from school, he would rush outside to see how his garden was getting on, and this year's developments promise to be even more exciting.

JENNIFER'S GARDEN

Jennifer is nine and has been gardening for six years. Of course, in the early days it was a matter of sowing sweet peas and sunflower seeds under supervision, but her interest has never dwindled. Since her family moved house two years ago she has had a good-sized garden of her own, about 3m × 1m (10ft × 3ft 6in). It has an old holly tree to one side and she has recently planted a small fir tree.

Jennifer is growing a mixture of flowers, fruit and vegetables. When she was younger she liked planting mixed random colours but now enjoys planning colour schemes. In spring there are irises, primroses, snowdrops, daffodils, yellow and white crocuses and tulips. The tulips are arranged yellow and red in a pattern. She particularly loves bright colours and last year she bought seedlings of dahlias, petunias and French marigolds which looked very lively. She also started some seeds off indoors using an ingenious device of her own invention: she took transparent egg cartons and used them for growing seeds, as though in a mini-greenhouse. One seed was planted in each compartment of the carton in a little bed of seed compost. Then the lid was closed and the seeds shot ahead much faster than they would have done without this protection. Last year she started sweet peas off this way and eventually produced an effective show at the back of the garden. She also planted a loganberry up the fence and has great hopes for this year. Then she grew some small bush tomatoes which were all eaten even before they got to the house. In addition she grew some herbs including basil and thyme.

This year Jennifer has enlarged the garden to include a private picnic area to which she can invite her friends. Again she is growing sweet peas and will buy other seedlings. She has also sown rudbeckia for its bright yellow colours and will get some more dahlias. Her father has promised some sweet Williams and some Michaelmas daisies.

CAROLINE'S GARDEN

Caroline is eleven years old and has been gardening since about the age of three when she showed herself very adept at planting vegetables. Her present garden is pretty big, so requires a lot of work, especially weeding. It stretches about 8m × 3m (26ft × 10ft) and contains a number of established shrubs, including a witch hazel, a cotoneaster and a cornus. She also has some old-fashioned pink roses which she grew from cuttings with help from her mother and a profusion of spring flowers – violets, primroses and bulbs including snowdrops, daffodils and various tulips.

She has laid a path of stepping stones across the garden made out of oval-shaped bricks and arranged in such a way as to make a round shape. It's not a regimented design but instead rather romantic-looking. One length of the garden is bordered by a garden path, the other by the lawn. At this juncture they have had to erect a low fence to stop the tortoise coming in – there was a sad death in the family a while back when a previous tortoise ate poisonous foxglove leaves. The fence also keeps the pet rabbit out.

Caroline has grown some successful vegetables in recent years including potatoes, radish, tomatoes, carrots, an amusing wigwam of climbing beans, and also a selection of herbs. She loves pumpkins because of their magic qualities but feels that they take up too much space, so she grows them in her parents' vegetable garden.

Her ambition is to make her garden more of a wildlife garden. The elderberries that landed there by chance have been left to sprout and form small trees. The native foxglove, primrose and violet thrive and she hopes to grow many wild flowers from seed. This year she is going to get a bird-table and is looking forward to seeing which birds are attracted into her garden.

AUGUSTIN'S GARDEN

Augustin lives in Dorset, a very rural part of England, where his family have a large garden. Both his parents are keen gardeners and he has had his own little garden since he was five. It stands about 2m × 2m (6ft × 6ft), isolated in the vegetable patch; a picturesque little oasis and a world of its own complete with its small pond. A path meanders across the centre so that he can tend the plants without treading on them.

The composition is charming. The tiny pool has a plastic bottom and there is a rock in the middle, home of a stone rabbit. Despite its small size the pool is regularly visited by frogs. When I saw it in spring there was a primrose flowering by the side. Later in the year there are foxgloves and forget-me-nots, a fuchsia, a white hydrangea and an interesting tall grass which adds texture. The rockery has small rock plants and an ornamental hedgehog on top.

Now Augustin is twelve and as he has grown older this little garden has not provided nearly enough scope, so he has expanded his gardening enterprises. At school he has a garden which he shares with four other boys. He does the lion's share of the work and they do more of the supplying. As he wanted this garden to be different from his own and as it was only temporary he put most of it over to vegetables, growing potatoes, radish, marrows, beans and peas.

He also helps his parents in the rest of the garden at home, specialising particularly in mowing and scything. He is fascinated by machinery which is handy as he hopes to be a farmer one day. Another big enterprise has been making a wild woodland garden with his father on a steep slope leading down to a stream. The wood has been thinned of scrub and they have laid paths using logs from felled trees. A boggy marsh was dug out to make a shallow natural pond for insects and tadpoles. Bluebells, ferns, primroses, anemones and other woodland flowers make this a very natural-looking wonderland.

As if this was not enough, Augustin's latest enterprise is to hire himself out in the school holidays as a jobbing gardener. He loves using a rotavator and spends whole days doing heavy work for neighbours. When he arrives home in the evening he's always longing for work to start again the next day.

SECRET GARDENS

'It was the sweetest, most mysterious-looking place
anyone could imagine. The high walls which shut it in
were covered with the leafless stems of climbing roses,
which were so thick they were matted together.'

'She did not want it to be a quite dead garden. If it were
a quite alive garden, how wonderful it would be, and
what thousands of roses would grow on every side.'

THE SECRET GARDEN

SECRET GARDENS

'There was every joy on earth in the secret garden that morning.'

I must have been about nine years old when I first read *The Secret Garden*, but I shall never forget my excitement. It became quite my favourite book and I read it again and again. Reading it once more when I was grown up I found that I had completely forgotten the plot and the characters. All that I could remember – and that very vividly indeed – was the heroine Mary (myself, of course) coming across the secret door in the wall almost hidden by ivy, somehow magically finding the key and opening the door into an enchanted, secret world full of excitement and surprises. Still, in my mind's eye, I can see the door with the glimpse of a beautiful, sunny little garden behind it.

In fact a lot more happened than that. The garden quite changed Mary's life, bringing her for the first time in touch with nature and the excitement of growth: 'If I have a spade,' she whispered, 'I can make the earth nice and soft and dig up weeds. If I have seeds and can make flowers grow, the garden won't be dead at all – it will come alive.' And she made her first young friend Dickon who shared her secret with her. It turned her from a selfish, 'contrary' girl who did not even like herself into a thoughtful and loving person. And once she had changed herself she set out to reform the extremely unpleasant boy Colin. So *The Secret Garden* has a lot to tell us all. At one level it is an enchanting story for children; at another it is a fable about man and his relationship with nature. Nature and the garden bring out the best in our characters and I am sure that this is true in real life as well as in fiction.

The reason this apparently old-fashioned tale is still so popular is that children do not change. They all love secrets and hidden things – whether it is my daughter's house under the dining-room table where no parents are allowed or a secret garden. They love to create private worlds that have as little to do with adults as possible. They also love surprises. So a secret place that is constantly changing, producing tiny bulb shoots in spring and rosebuds in summer, is irresistible.

Once she had found her garden Mary set about putting it to rights since it had been neglected for ten years. 'She went from place to place, and dug and weeded, and enjoyed herself so immensely that she was led on from bed to bed and into the grass under the trees.' Of course she got tips from Ben Weatherstaff, the gruff old gardener, and her new friend Dickon. But the fact that the children did it all themselves, weeding and pruning and sowing seeds and transforming the garden from a wilderness to something beautiful again makes it so much more exciting. 'They ran from one part of the garden to another and found so many wonders that they were obliged to remind themselves that they must whisper or speak low. He showed her swelling leaf-buds on rose branches that seemed dead. He showed her ten thousand new green points pushing through the mould.'

The really magic person in *The Secret Garden* is Dickon. This boy from across the moors can talk to birds and animals and has a pet fox and a pet crow. Martha, his sister, says, 'He's got sheep on th' moor that knows him, an' birds as comes an' eats out of his hand.' He seems to Mary like some 'sort of wood fairy who might be gone when she came into the garden again'. Getting to know animals and talking to them is what we all dream about as children, and it is only when Mary begins to talk to the robin that you feel she is capable of loving anything. When he came close 'she was so happy that she scarcely dared to breathe'.

Having said all this, how do you make a secret garden today? Many gardens are not nearly big enough to allow you to create a special enclosed area. If you have the space then it really is fun and worth doing, but if not just do your best to make your own small garden seem as secret as you can.

So what are the ingredients that go to make a successful secret garden? First, it must be a surprise. If possible its entrance should be hidden from view either because it is a very narrow gap in a hedge or the entry is concealed by some bush or tree. And it's best if there is only one entrance to it. A gate in a wall would be ideal, but it's by no means necessary.

Secondly, it must be enclosed and extremely private with high surrounding hedges or a fence. There is nothing secret about a garden if parents are going to pop their heads over the fence all the time. In our garden we are lucky enough to have high walls, so we are planning a secret garden in one corner. There is already a large box bush which hides that area from the house and we are transferring some quite mature yew bushes to fill up the fourth side of the square, leaving a tiny gap to squeeze through. We are doing this now while our children are small so that it will be the right height for them in five years or so when they come to use it regularly.

So you should erect a good bit of wooden fencing or plant a hedge if there is time. Personally I much prefer the hedge idea because it gives the birds a chance to nest in the garden. Box is very slow-growing, so try yew or a deciduous hedge of beech or hornbeam. Avoid Leyland cypress which keen and thoughtless nurserymen will try to sell you: they are very dull, grow extremely fast and you will be clipping for ever.

ROSES

The Secret Garden was described as 'The sweetest, most mysterious-looking place anyone could imagine'. So now you have the structure, set about making it just that. The most important flowers in the garden were roses: when Mary first entered she noticed that 'The high walls which shut it in were covered with the leafless stems of climbing roses, which were so thick they were matted together.' Roses are the most romantic flowers. Children love their appearance and perfume and most modern roses, and quite a few of the old ones, will last all summer through – with a slight pause for breath in the middle. Grow climbing roses up the wall or fence or even into the hedge. Think of making a rose arch over the entrance to the secret garden which will make it look even more enchanted. There are a vast number of varieties you can choose but here are a few suggestions.

'Golden Showers' is a really pretty bright yellow, flowers most of the summer and is also good for picking. Vivid pink 'Zéphirine Drouhin' flowers very early, then spasmodically, and has the advantage for children that it does not have any thorns. (It is probably best to avoid extremely thorny roses like 'Albertine' which is otherwise so very lovely with its soft coral flowers and sweet apple scent.) 'Mermaid' is a delightful open yellow rose which flowers throughout the summer, but it is not good for picking.

As a child I was particularly fond of 'New Dawn' which we grew over our porch. It has very soft light pink flowers and flowers all summer and its lovely scent filled the rooms nearby. 'Mme Grégoire Staechelin' is a larger, more vivid pink. It lasts a long time and has the advantage of flourishing on a north wall.

Rambler roses with their hundreds of tiny little flowers are very romantic and seem particularly appropriate to secret gardens though they only have one flowering season. 'Félicité et Perpétue' is an enchanting rose if you can get hold of it and produces a mass of little pinky white double flowers. 'Dorothy Perkins' is a famous bright pink rambler which will soon look as if it is growing wild and so will 'Excelsa' or 'Crimson Shower', both a vivid crimson colour. Finally I love 'Phyllis Bide' with its succession of tiny yellowy pink flowers all summer long.

With all these roses climbing up the wall you might choose not to have rose bushes as well, and anyway there may not be room. But it would be fun to grow a few of the numerous kinds of miniature roses. You might also grow my favourite rose from childhood: 'The Fairy'. This enchanting bush flowers most of the summer and well into the autumn, bearing many sprays of small sugar-pink flowers which are straight out of a bridesmaid's posy.

FLOWERS AND HERBS

There are so many different flowers that children can grow and I list a lot of them in Chapter 5. However, for a secret garden it is best to choose those that do not need a great deal of looking after as parents will not be around to give assistance. I would suggest it is a very good place to grow herbs like lavender, sage, rue, rosemary, tansy and thyme which can be cut and brought indoors to make lavender bags or enhance the cooking.

Bulbs need very little attention and in *The Secret Garden* it is the bulbs that tell Mary that spring is on the way: 'There were things sprouting and pushing out from the roots of clumps of plants and there were actually here and there glimpses of royal purple and yellow unfurling among the stems of crocuses.' She sees their tiny shoots coming up through the earth and starts clearing away all the weeds to give them room to breathe. I've listed many bulbs in Chapter 5 and some smaller ones in the chapter on miniature gardens, and I recommend them wholeheartedly. Start with snowdrops then progress to crocuses, daffodils, scillas and irises and the children will have something to pick for posies from the end of the winter onwards.

COLOUR SCHEMES

In Elizabethan times the big formal gardens were made up of lots of smaller gardens divided by hedges. They loved to have their gardens full of secrets and surprises so went in for hidden rooms and mazes where you could get lost. Then these gardens went out of fashion. In this century gardens like Sissinghurst and Hidcote went back to the idea of having a number of different gardens like separate rooms in a house, each with a particular character. The famous white garden at Sissinghurst is a good example which many people have copied.

It might be great fun to grow flowers of a particular colour in your secret garden, making it different from the rest of the garden. White is an obvious example as you can grow beautiful silver-leaved plants as well as white flowers, but children tend to prefer bright colours. You need not use only one colour but a combination – red, orange and yellow, for example. Blue and yellow is another very attractive colour scheme, or you might go for pink and white or blue, mauve and pink. The children could be involved in choosing the different flowers – a good way of learning flower names. Certainly I as a child was fascinated by flower colours and enjoyed evolving my own colour patterns – luckily, in nature you don't often get dreadful clashes of colour. So here are some suggestions: it is by no means a long list but is meant to act as a jumping off point.

A golden garden

Flowers in this garden would be yellow and orange and you would also go for plants with yellow or variegated yellow leaves such as climbing ivy 'Goldheart' and the glossy evergreen shrub *Elaeagnus pungens*. In spring grow winter jasmine and gold-flowered kerria up the wall and bulbs such as crocuses, aconites, daffodils and narcissi, irises and anemones in the beds. Then there are polyanthus, primroses, cowslips and some gold-leaved heathers. The brightest bush of spring is yellow forsythia. In early summer soft yellow and deeper gold wallflowers will overlap with the later tulips and daffodils.

In summer yellow roses will bloom on the walls. The first, in a sheltered spot, could be *R. banksiae lutea* with its tiny pom pom flowers, later 'Mermaid', 'Golden Showers' and 'Allgold'. Good shrubs are the yellow-leafed *Philadelphus* 'Aureus' which has scented white flowers and yellow-flowered hypericum. There are countless yellow summer flowers to choose from, but my suggestions would include antirrhinum, pansy and viola, begonia, dahlia, calendula, achillea, limnanthes (poached egg plant), chrysanthemum, gazania, lily, lupin, marigold, petunia, helichrysum, nasturtium, poppy, tagetes, tall verbascum and finally the giant sunflower. Many of these would carry on flowering until autumn when the walls should hang with the enchanting lantern flowers of *Clematis tangutica*.

A sapphire garden

Blue has always been my favourite colour and blue flowers have first place in my garden. This garden would contain blue and mauve flowers starting in spring with bulbs like scilla, *Anemone blanda*, muscari, chionodoxa, *Iris reticulata*, crocus, hyacinth and bluebell plants like forget-me-not and polyanthus. Come summer the walls would bloom with ceanothus and other climbers like ipomoea (morning glory) and *Cobaea scandens* easily grown from seed. There are many blue and mauve clematis such as little *C. macropetala* and the larger-flowered *C.* 'Jackmanii'. Small shrubs like lavender and rosemary have lovely blue flowers and later the beautiful shrub caryopteris. Rue has vivid blue leaves and some silver-leaved plants would mix well here.

In high summer there are lots of blue flowers. Here are a few suggestions: anchusa, campanula, Canterbury bells, ageratum, lobelia, cornflower, love-

in-a-mist, salvia, sweet pea, pansy and viola, larkspur, cynoglossum, delphinium and finally the amazing blue thistles called echinops.

A ruby garden

This garden requires more care because even in nature reds can clash. Vivid scarlet salvias will scream at crimson roses, for example, so do a bit of research before you begin. I have selected a mixture of red and pink plants and the effect could be stunning. Plant copper-leaved shrubs of which there are many: try some berberis or tiny acer trees and copper-coloured varieties of weigela and pittosporum. On the walls grow red-berried shrubs like pyracantha and cotoneaster and, of course, roses. Good climbing roses are 'Parkdirektor Riggers' and 'Zéphirine Drouhin'. The best rose shrub is the red-leaved rose *R. rubrifolia* which has pink flowers and red hips.

Spring is short on red flowers but there are some lovely pink bulbs like chionodoxa and hyacinth and all shades of tulips. Later the vivid reds and pinks of the wallflowers will overlap with the late tulips. Come summer there are many more flowers to choose from including geraniums, pinks and carnations, hollyhocks, celosia (Prince of Wales feathers), cosmea, dahlia, begonia, salvia, sweet William, valerian, zinnia, lavatera, nicotiana, nasturtium, helichrysum, petunia, poppy, penstemon, lupin, antirrhinum and of course a huge selection of different colours and shades of sweet pea.

A diamond garden

White gardens have become very popular, so when planning yours you might be able to go and look at another one first. The important thing is to have lovely silver leaves alongside the white flowers. Good silver shrubs are *Senecio greyi,* several varieties of artemisia and santolina (cotton lavender). Many shrubs have white flowers such as philadelphus, choisya and all kinds of viburnum. Up the walls you can grow climbers starting with lovely *Clematis armandii* which flowers in early spring. Later there are many other kinds of white clematis such as *C.* henryi, *C.* 'Marie Boisselot' and *C. balearica*. Another wonderful white climber is *Hydrangea petiolaris* and there is also a marvellous white wisteria. Climbing white roses include rampant 'Wedding Day', 'Mrs Honey Dyson', pretty pom pom flowered 'Albéric Barbier' and many more. There are also climbing versions of the roses 'Iceberg' and 'Pascali' which are a must in a white garden.

Spring has numerous white flowers starting with snowdrops, then anemone, some narcissi, crocus, hyacinth, iris, muscari and tulips. In summer there are many more, among them geranium, alyssum, antirrhinum, gypsophila, lavatera, dahlia, begonia, nicotiana, impatiens, candytuft, white foxgloves, petunia, pansy and viola, sweet pea, lily, iris and *Chrysanthemum maximum*. Then of course there are those flowers which also have silver foliage – carnations, pinks and finally cerastium which will grow in heavenly clumps along the ground and is better known as snow in summer.

FRUIT

Fruit trees are lovely, both for their blossom in spring and their fruits in autumn. It is particularly nice for children to be able to grow their own fruit as in the original secret garden. As there probably won't be much space I suggest you think of growing a cordon apple, pear or plum against the wall or fence. These trees have the added advantage that children can reach the fruit without having to use a ladder. Other good climbing fruit are blackberries and loganberries. I am particularly fond of the thornless blackberry: it has leaves quite unlike the wild blackberry being rather spidery. It also grows very fast and produces a large quantity of delicious berries.

BIRDS

Dickon described the secret garden as 'the safest nestin' place in England'. All birds felt safe and even Mary's friend the robin built his nest there. Your secret garden should also be a haven for birds. For a start they will love to make nests in the hedge and they will happily eat those rose hips. The thicker the climbers on the wall or fence, the more likely they are to make good nesting-places.

But in addition this would be a good place to put nesting-boxes – they could be fixed to the wall or fence. Remember to put them up at the beginning of winter as some small birds may use them as a refuge long before they actually want to start laying eggs. In the centre of the garden, well out of the reach of cats, put a bird-table. Give it a roof if you can and be sure that in winter food is put on it regularly. Or you might hang a bird-feeder from an overhanging branch.

As I said at the start, most of us, particularly in town, don't have the luxury of enough space for a separate secret garden. But I hope that some of my suggestions might be useful and help you to make your own garden more like a secret garden. Buy a copy of the book if you don't have one already and let the whole family plan together.

MINIATURE GARDENS

'This doll's house garden was a magic land, a forest of flowers through which roamed creatures I had never seen before.'

'There was a whole landscape on this wall if you peered closely enough to see it; the roofs of a hundred tiny toadstools, red, yellow and brown, showed in patches like villages on the damper portions; a mountain of bottle-green moss grew in tuffets so symmetrical that they might have been planted and trimmed; forests of small ferns sprouted from cracks in the shady places, drooping languidly like little green fountains.'

MY FAMILY AND OTHER ANIMALS

MINIATURE GARDENS

MINIATURE gardens are fun for everyone, whatever the size of your garden. If you have only a patio or a windowsill, then obviously there isn't much alternative. But even if you have lots of space, there is something very exciting about making a garden of tiny plants – as if you were creating a world entirely of your own with miniature paths, bridges, trees and even miniature people and animals.

The first miniature garden a child will make will probably be a tray garden. This is only a temporary affair but none the less exciting for that. Precisely because it is temporary and can be altered easily it is a wonderful exercise in design for a child.

A tray garden is a garden on an old tray made of moss and sand decorated with twigs, flowers and trinkets. The sand is to preserve the moisture and provide a firm base into which things can be stuck. First lay out the layer of sand, then create the design by decorating it, using moss to represent grass and mounds, twigs as trees, flowers, and perhaps silver paper to represent a pond. Shells and pebbles will add interest and you can put in miniature houses and people it with little animals or dolls. Tray gardens take up very little space, can be made indoors or out and provide endless pleasure.

Children can make a more permanent miniature garden in a specially designated flower-bed, but most gardens of this kind are more effective if they are made in troughs, old square sinks, large wooden boxes or even window boxes or tubs. This way they are isolated from the rest of the garden. If you choose to make your miniature garden indoors, you can grow indoor plants or miniature bulbs. Aged ten, I used to have an impressive indoor garden of cacti and succulents: it was about 75cm × 30cm (2ft 6in × 1ft) and lived quite close to a radiator near a window. It became extremely jungly in time and I introduced animals made in pottery class at school – giraffes, elephants etc. – to add to the wild effect.

Whether the garden is in a trough or a tub, it's crucial that it should have good drainage so the plants don't permanently have their feet in water. This is particularly important with the little alpine plants as they are accustomed to well-drained, sunny places. So first make sure that the trough has a hole or two in the bottom and second that water can get out of the holes. This means that the trough should be slightly raised at one end. Fill the bottom quarter of the trough with pebbles or bits of broken plant pots and cover this with an old cloth, piece of sacking or anything which will stop earth getting through while allowing water to drain away. Then fill the rest of the trough with a good, peaty compost which will hold water well, or a mixture of soil and compost. Leaving 2cm ($\frac{5}{8}$in) or so at the top of the trough, firm the soil down. Now you are ready to plant. Remember that troughs can easily dry out, so they must be watered very regularly in summer. Lastly, if the trough can be raised up it will be much easier to work on. If you have a low wall or ledge, that would be an ideal place to position your miniature garden.

A ROCK PLANT GARDEN

Most outdoor miniature gardens feature rock plants. I list a selection on pages 131–2 but there are obviously hundreds to choose from and a good nursery garden should be able to advise. The only rule is to choose plants that will not spread too fast – purple alyssum, for example, would be hopeless. Even if you choose very tiny plants you may have to divide them up in due course and pass on your surplus to friends. Remember that rock plants need lots of sun so place the trough in the brightest spot before you fill it with earth and make it too heavy to move. I'm afraid that neither rock plants nor miniature bulbs come cheap, but at least your space is limited and you might be able to get some bits and pieces from neighbours' gardens or your own.

First decide on the shape of your garden just as if you were planning a large garden. Include some rocks to give it an interesting structure and maybe some shells picked up on summer holidays. There could also be a meandering path of pebbles and an expensive but exciting addition would be a miniature tree. Personally I am not keen on bonsai trees – and they cost the earth – but the genuine dwarf conifers which are to be found in many garden centres can look lovely in a trough whereas I think they look out of place in a big garden. They come in various shades of evergreen and are so bright and cheerful in winter, making your garden colourful all year round.

Junipers are interesting conifers. The dwarf variety ideal for tubs is *J. communis* which is an upright conical shape with deep green foliage. *J. × media Pfitzerana Aurea* has a yellow leaf and would spread over the edge. Later on, it might need a bit of clipping back.

Cypress (*Chamaecyparis*) come in many dwarf varieties, though some may eventually grow a bit large for a tub and will have to be cut back or moved – two of the smallest ones are *C. obtusa* 'Nana' *graintis* which has a bright green bushy shape and *thyoides* 'Ericoides' which turns bronze in winter. 'Minima Aurea' is conical with bright gold foliage.

Picea or spruce also make charming rock garden trees. The type that will stay small enough for tubs is *Picea glauca* 'Nana' which forms a low round bush growing eventually to about a foot.

Thuja is a cone-shaped bush which comes in many varieties. The dwarf sort like *Thuya orientalis* 'Aurea Nana' is golden-coloured and rarely reaches over 30cm (12in).

Miniature Rock Plants

Armeria (or thrift) Makes tufts of tiny pink flowers in mid-summer.

Campanula The dwarf form *C. cochleariifolia* will spill over the edge in sky blue clumps.

Dianthus (or pinks) These flower in little clumps all summer long. The alpine varieties all stay small but will trail over the tub edge.

Erinus alpinus This forms delightful clumps of bright pink, red or white flowers.

Gentiana Gentians can be too large, but some varieties like *G. verna* will stay small. This has vivid blue horn-shaped flowers.

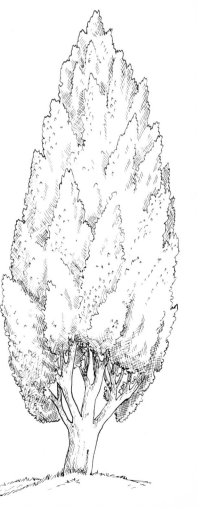

Phlox The *douglasii* varieties have clumps of tiny brilliant flowers blooming in early summer.

Saxifrage Avoid the spreading varieties, but many such as the Krabschia group, *S. xapiculata*, *S. cochlearis* 'Minor', and *S. haagii*, will form neat enchanting clumps of pinks, whites and yellows in spring.

Sedum These have thick, rather cactus-like leaves which hold a lot of water and clusters of flat pink flowers. The tiny varieties like *S. album* and *lydium* are ideal.

Sempervivum These have leaves similar to sedum. Nearly all varieties have a strong smell and look attractive throughout the year forming cactus-like clumps.

A MINIATURE ROSE GARDEN

Miniature roses are lovely things and they come in as great a variety of colours as ordinary roses, but this is a garden that would only look interesting in summer. You could make a very small one in a trough or in a special flower-bed. Remember that rose gardens are rather formal affairs. If you are lucky enough to have one locally, all go to look at it, to get ideas.

The most famous rose garden, which was copied all over the world, is the Roseraie de l'Hay near Paris. This has a marvellous pattern of paths with pergolas and arches reaching down them and beds in between. Statues and fountains are positioned at the end of vistas or the centre of roped archways, and there are seats in the rose bowers so visitors can sit and smell the roses in the evening. Obviously you will incorporate only some of these ingredients, but the overall effect should be formal. Paths can be made of shells or pebbles.

Remember that roses should be fed regularly in summer if they are to flower a lot, so compost will not be enough. Instead, a liquid fertiliser mixed in with the water periodically will make a big difference. Miniature roses do not need severe pruning, but encourage dead-heading during the summer. Then in early spring cut them back to a good shape snipping off the straggly stems.

Miniature Roses

'Cinderella' is an enchanting double white flower with a blush of pink.

'New Penny' has superb, glossy foliage and bright red flowers.

'Rosina' is always recommended as the best of the yellow miniatures.

'Yellow Doll' is a good bright yellow.

'Starina' produces a host of bright orange-scarlet flowers over a long period.

'Sweet Fairy' is one of the tiniest miniatures. It has many soft, light pink flowers which seem to have hundreds of petals.

'Baby Masquerade' is a very exciting mix. Its buds appear bright red and then open out to a clear yellow.

'Pour Toi' has many beautifully formed white blooms. It is very vigorous and free-flowering.

'Royal Salute' is a very bright pink double rose. It is one of the most popular miniatures because it flowers all summer.

A MINIATURE BULB GARDEN

Miniature bulbs can be grown alongside the rock plants in a small rock garden, but you can also devote your whole garden to spring bulbs. This would have a shorter life as bulbs die back once they have flowered and then don't appear again for another year, but planting and planning a bulb garden is an interesting autumn job. If the garden is made in a small container, then it can be brought indoors so the bulbs will bloom before their relatives outside.

Remember that it is important to plant bulbs in clumps of a particular kind – a daffodil on its own looks silly, but a group of five looks very natural. And bear in mind the eventual height the bulbs will grow to – a good catalogue will give you a fair idea.

Try and make the garden look like something – a woodland glade with a stream going through or a dell with a little pond, for example. A mirror with its edges concealed by earth is a popular way of indicating a pond. Perhaps a few animals like rabbits, frogs, hedgehogs or foxes would be playing there in spring, and you might also add a little bridge. Some interestingly shaped bits of dead wood to indicate trees and tree stumps would look pretty and maybe a large rock by the pool, firmly embedded in the soil. This will give a good framework to the garden.

You could kick off with a clump of early snowdrops and perhaps some yellow aconites before any of the other bulbs appear. Then a few miniature narcissi would look lovely: the variety called *N. minimus* is a tiny 7.5cm (3in) daffodil with a long trumpet. 'Tete-a-Tete' grows around 12.5cm (5in) and has petals that fold back like a cyclamen while *N. cyclamineus* has petals which fold back completely with a long trumpet and grows around 15cm (6in). Then there is a sweet little variety called *N. juncifolius* (the miniature rush-leaved daffodil) growing 10cm (4in) and the bright 'Yellow Hoop Petticoat' with an enormous cup which grows 15cm (6in).

Tiny crocuses will look pretty, particularly if you choose the small species varieties and avoid the larger Dutch ones. Most tulips are far too tall but some of the kaufmanniana hybrids grow to about 15cm (6in) and then there are little species tulips like my own great favourite, the buttercup yellow *Tulipa tarda* which is even smaller.

Other possibilities are little *Anemone blanda* with its delicate bushy leaves and daisy-like flowers in blue, white and pink, which grow to around 12.5cm (5in); tiny blue or white chionodoxa; muscari or grape hyacinth which look pretty in a clump of blue, and also the enchanting deep blue scillas with their bell-like flowers which grow 10cm (4in) tall. Finally, perhaps beside the pond, little *Iris reticulata* could look like a wild flag. These come in shades of yellow, purple, blue and white, are very exciting to look at and stop at about 15cm (6in).

A MIXED MINIATURE GARDEN

So far I have dealt with rock gardens, rose gardens and bulb gardens separately, but there is no reason why you should not mix your plants. Do remember, however, that only the tiniest bulbs will be anything like as small as the rock plants. Miniature daffodils, crocuses and tulips might rather swamp them and look out of proportion.

Having said that, this mixed garden might attempt to look like your family garden in miniature. Don't try to copy it to scale as the bushes would all look too small, but the general shape – the position of the house, pond, play area, terrace, paths and so on – could be the same. A small wooden box painted in waterproof paint could represent the house.

It is impossible to grow grass on such a small scale so keep the lawn area down to a minimum and use moss – if you live in a country with a damp climate you won't have any trouble finding a supply. In most English homes there's far too much of it in the lawn not to mention in the walls and on the roof of the house, so a good collection could be made and planted flat on the soil. It can be cut back regularly with scissors.

Sand, gravel and small stones can represent the terrace, paths and play area, and miniature swings and slides can easily be made or bought. Build a little sandpit, a gate, a fence and a garden shed too. Again, rocks and shells add interest and somewhere there might be a pool. Miniature roses and dwarf conifers will represent trees and bushes and choose a few alpine plants with perhaps clumps of bulbs like scillas and chionodoxa for the flower-beds.

Another good idea would be to make a farmhouse country garden. This would give you scope for a farmyard with a good selection of animals as well as a garden and an orchard.

MINIATURE HERB GARDENS

Most children enjoy being able to contribute to the family meal from their gardens. And a herb garden – which need only be in a large tub, though it could occupy a substantial box – is an ideal way for them to do this. Remember herbs need a lot of sun, so a position on a south-facing patio would be best. But you could instead grow your herbs on a windowsill in a special herb pot or strawberry pot, a cylindrical or oval shape, usually in terracotta, with holes at intervals in the side. This is filled with earth and has different herbs growing out of each hole. Many herbs can easily be grown from seed and then transferred to the garden, so this is quite an inexpensive enterprise. If the garden is in a low box that would fit on a deep window ledge, it could be brought inside and provide herbs for winter salads as well.

The traditional full-scale herb garden which the Elizabethans loved was a very formal garden divided up in intricate patterns. Obviously a small-scale garden cannot be too fiddly, but a criss-cross of paths could be laid down with perhaps a statue or miniature sundial in the middle to give the same elegant effect. Most herbs will have to be cut back regularly or they will get very crowded, but there is no harm in this as once chopped they can go straight into the salad or the soup. But do avoid the larger herbs such as lovage, fennel, mint and sorrel.

The obvious herb to start with is thyme: this grows into a charming little evergreen bush which can be chopped back to a good shape. The sort you will buy in a seed packet is common thyme which is deep green and bears tiny purple flowers, but herb farmers and nurseries can supply plants of variegated, golden and silver thyme to add variety. Marjoram is another useful small herb which comes in green and golden varieties and grows in pretty clumps. More statuesque is evergreen rosemary of which you might grow a small bush for some years before transferring it to a larger garden. Sage – green, golden or red – similarly forms a good small shrub if kept trim. Chives are easily grown and are a boon in any kitchen. Parsley is temperamental but will look attractive if you succeed. Tarragon and basil are annual tender herbs which can be grown from seed for summer cooking but tarragon can become quite unwieldy. The seed packets will give instructions about how to sow in spring and summer.

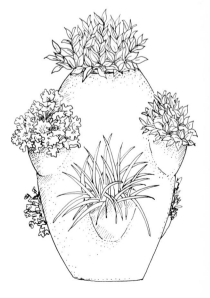

INDOOR MINIATURE GARDENS

These are particularly important if a child lives in a flat and does not have the chance to have an outdoor garden. But even if there is lots of outdoor space, indoor gardens provide interest and entertainment in winter as well as looking extremely pretty. Have a trough built to fit a particular window ledge or just use a large attractive bowl with lots of pebbles or crocks in the bottom to avoid overwatering. Remember that the air in most houses is very dry so – with the exception of cacti – most indoor plants would welcome a regular spray. A fine water sprayer is an essential piece of equipment.

A CACTI AND SUCCULENT GARDEN

Cacti hold a particular fascination for children. Their strange shapes and sharp spines are very weird and wonderful and sometimes they have the added bonus of producing flowers. What's more, they need very little care and don't mind dry conditions as this is what they are accustomed to in the wild deserts where they come from.

Cacti look most natural surrounded by pebbles and stones, so fill your tub or trough with crocks and soil up to about 4cm ($1\frac{1}{2}$in) from the top. Take time designing the garden, using a variety of shapes to provide interesting contrasts – put a tree-like *Rhipsalis cereuscula* near the rotund, spiky oroya and the coryphantha which looks like a pile of stones.

Once the cacti are planted, water them and then cover the soil with a 1cm ($\frac{1}{2}$in) layer of pebbles. You can buy quite attractive ones from aquarium shops. You might also add some boulder-like stones to make your garden look more like a desert.

There are hosts of cacti to choose from and it is worth looking at an illustrated guide for the whole range. But I would suggest *Crassula argentea* which spreads like a spongey-leafed tree, and opuntia, or prickly pear, which grows many pear-shaped stems in small curving spikes – both this and cereus look as though they come straight out of Wild West films. I am also fascinated by the stone-like argyroderma and the tall cephalo-

cereus which is covered with furry spines like matted grey hair. The smaller round varieties like ferocactus are simply covered in spines as are the round oroya. The hawarthia has rosettes of thick, fleshy leaves with white and green markings. They spread easily producing babies at their side which you can pot and give to friends. Mine have successfully flowered indoors.

A HOUSEPLANT GARDEN

As with cacti it's worth doing a lot of research before buying plants for a houseplant garden, but luckily there are lots of good, cheap books on the subject. It's crucial not to plant plants such as aspidistra or philadendum which will soon swamp their neighbours. Instead look out for attractive trailing plants which can hang over the edge of your tub.

You should aim to achieve a mixture of colours and shapes which will both contrast with and complement each other. Fortunately many indoor plants have fascinating coloured leaves; obvious examples are the begonias (but choose a small variety) and the brilliantly striped calathea. The popular spider plant (chlorophytum) has many thin, striped, yellow and green leaves and mixes attractively. It produces tiny new plants on stems which you can pot up and give away. Another brilliant leaf is coleus which comes in many shades of red, yellow and green, all variegated, though this will eventually grow too large and have to be transferred to a pot.

The charming little flat green leaves of fittonia have intricate white markings on the veins. This is a creeping plant and is excellent for edging. So is helxine, better known as mind-your-own-business, whose thousands of tiny green and gold leaves look just like a carpet and would make an excellent centre to a garden. Tradescantia is an attractive variegated hanging plant which grows voraciously and must be controlled.

In contrast to these more succulent leaves grow a fern or two. The charming adiantum or maidenhair fern is soft lime green and very delicate. A polypodium, on the other hand, is much sturdier.

Into this jungly-looking garden you might put a pond and perhaps some model animals and birds who would like the surroundings enough to make their homes there.

TERRARIUMS

These are miniature gardens created in bottles or glass tanks, so all the moisture that evaporates from the soil or plants returns to them. The Victorians were particularly fond of them and called them Wardian cases after Mr Ward who invented them. Plants lived for years in these controlled environments, growing ever wilder. Some of the more elaborate cases looked like miniature greenhouses; you can still buy these today but they are extremely expensive. A cheaper alternative is a fish tank plus a glass top, or possibly a large round bottle.

First buy a bag of potting compost and some pebbles, then select a mixture of smallish but interestingly contrasting houseplants to form the arrangement. As it is crucial that no diseases enter the terrarium at this stage, I suggest standing it with the pebbles in some sterilising solution (like the sort used for babies' bottles) overnight. Then clean the container and cover the bottom with a layer of pebbles about 2.5cm (1in) thick. To stop the compost mixing with the pebbles, put a layer of muslin or old

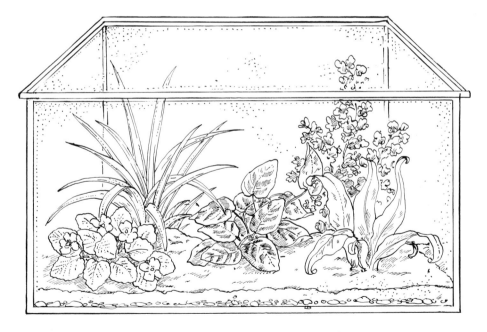

cotton over the pebbles and then add your bed of compost. In a tank this is quite simple but for a bottle you will need a funnel for the soil and a pair of long sticks to arrange things, using them like chop sticks.

Now water the compost quite thoroughly remembering that any excess water will drain through to the layer of pebbles, preventing the compost from becoming waterlogged. Then carefully arrange the plants according to your design, perhaps adding some decorative shells, stones or ornaments to add some variety. Finally seal the top and place the terrarium in a light, warmish place.

There are many, many variations on this simple suggestion. I have even seen a large coffee table made of a terrarium. But whatever you create I think you will find your miniature jungle as exciting and mysterious as I found mine and you will be particularly glad of it in the winter when there's nothing to be done in the garden outside.

YOUR GARDEN NATURE RESERVE

'At first I was so bewildered by this profusion of life on
our very doorstep that I could only move about the
garden in a daze, watching now this creature, now that,
constantly having my attention distracted by the flights
of brilliant butterflies that drifted over the hedge.
Gradually, as I became more used to the bustle of insect
life among the flowers, I found I could concentrate more.
I would spend hours squatting on my heels or lying on
my stomach watching the private lives of the creatures
around me . . . . In this way I learnt a lot of fascinating
things.'

MY FAMILY AND OTHER ANIMALS

YOUR GARDEN NATURE RESERVE

ADULTS have an annoying way of saying that things were better when they were children. But where birds and butterflies are concerned, this is certainly true. I remember going every spring with my mother to inspect a long patch of gorse bushes which ran along the side of the narrow lane leading to our house. It was full of birds' nests and she would lift me up to examine them, first when the eggs were laid – we had a book so could identify the song thrush, robin, wren and so on – and later when the baby birds had hatched and were feeding. When the birds had flown we would dissect a nest on the lawn finding the amazing mix of cotton, sheep's wool, grass and straw that made up the beautifully built home. It was incredibly exciting. Then somebody in a distant office decided that our narrow lane should be widened. One summer, along came the bulldozers and destroyed all those gorse bushes, without so much as a by-your-leave to the birds whose regular home they had been.

Hedges have similarly disappeared in many countries: in Europe farmers are paid government money to sow more wheat and they don't think twice before removing an ancient hedge – the home of birds, insects and animals for hundreds of years – just to claim the extra money. And many woodlands, the other traditional habitat of animals and birds, have been cut down to make way for farms and houses.

However, nature is extraordinarily adaptable and the result of all these changes in the countryside is that those remaining birds and butterflies have got used to using gardens as their homes. By encouraging them in you are not only creating your own fascinating nature reserve – you are also doing them a service. But how can you attract them into your garden? Obviously different birds and insects have different needs and I shall deal with their individual feeding habits separately, but they also have many needs in common.

145

Children are by nature conservationists. They have a natural curiosity for everything around them and love feeding birds, watching insects in a pond and butterflies in the flower-beds. By far the best story of a child's obsession with nature is Gerald Durrell's classic *My Family and Other Animals* which tells how he as a ten-year-old boy arrived with his family to live on the island of Corfu. It follows his journey of discovery and describes the menagerie of animals and insects he found there – the spiders, the owls, the scorpions and magpies, all of whom became pets at one time or another.

His particular bit of luck was meeting up with Theodore Stephanides, a learned naturalist who treated him as an equal and with whom, every Thursday, he would go on collecting expeditions.

> 'Every water-filled ditch or pool was, to us, a teeming and unexplored jungle. . . . Every hollow tree had to be closely observed . . . every mossy wigged rock had to be overturned to find out what lay beneath it, and every rotten log had to be dissected. Standing straight and immaculate at the edge of the pool, Theodore would carefully sweep his little net through the water, lift it out, and peer keenly into the tiny glass bottle that dangled at the end, into which all the minute water life had been sifted. "Ah ha!" he might say, his voice ringing with excitement, his beard bristling. "I believe it's *Ceriodaphnia laticaudata*."'

It was Theodore who gave Gerry that tool without which no naturalist can manage: a magnifying glass.

The wonderful thing about Gerald Durrell is that he has retained his childlike obsession with nature as a grown man. He founded and runs a zoo in Jersey where endangered species are bred. He pioneers for conservation and has written a marvellous reference book, *The Amateur Naturalist*. It is dedicated to Theodore and is intended to give today's young naturalists the same help and advice that he received from Theodore all those years ago. So you see, it is important to start young. Today many children's television programmes take an active part in studying nature and conservation and there are various societies (like Watch in Britain) which help children learn about conservation and run camps for keen naturalists.

As I have said already, I don't like a garden to look too regimented. I prefer it to look as though nature has been tamed just a bit, with lots of unexpected nooks and crannies for hide-and-seek. Luckily birds and insects feel the same. They prefer old-fashioned flowers which have stronger scents. They like bushes and hedges which provide shelter and woody, wild areas which resemble the natural countryside. The ideal wildlife garden should look like a woodland glade with long grasses at the edge full of wild flowers and a lot of shrubs which are native to the country you live in. It is worth knowing that native trees and shrubs will provide food and shelter for many more varieties of insects and animals than imported exotic trees and shrubs. When you think about it, it stands to reason that they should – a Japanese azalea does not come complete with Japanese insects and similarly an English oak, which will house over two hundred different kinds of invertebrate when growing in England, would not be nearly as useful in America. In Chapter 3 we drew a plan for a nature garden, including a mixed hedge of British shrubs like hawthorn, willow and elder. In other countries find out what your local shrubs are and plant a selection.

When we first moved to our present house my husband started mowing the long grass in the orchard and was very upset when a hedgehog got caught up in the mower and was killed. This just showed how necessary it was to have a wild area where nettles, wild flowers and long grasses could flourish and animals and insects feel at home. A hedgehog is such a friendly visitor to your garden and as he lives on slugs, beetles and worms, ignoring flowers and vegetables, it would be helpful if he stayed.

Many of us don't have a large enough garden for a wild area, but even in the middle of town the birds have got to nest and feed somewhere. You can still create a mini nature reserve by training thick climbers like ivy up your walls, growing berry fruit and the kind of flowers the bees will enjoy. Once birds know there is a source of food, water and shelter in your garden, it won't be long before they are breeding there.

The most important rule in a wildlife garden is not to use poisons. Chemicals that kill plants and pests can also kill the other insects, animals and birds that feed on them. People have gardened for hundreds of years without using chemicals and there are many less harmful but equally effective remedies: remove weeds by hoeing or spray aphids with a mixture of water and soap flakes. Chemicals are not all necessarily harmful, but while a manufacturer may point out on the label that one particular substance is dangerous for pets, he may well neglect to mention wildlife. Remember that many so-called weeds are the most lovely wild flowers and you should not risk losing them. Others like nettles are in fact essential to some butterflies.

I shall name some common birds and animals you may attract to your garden, but the possibilities are endless and depend greatly on the area you live in. So it's definitely worth buying an authoritative bird book and a butterfly book giving full descriptions with colour pictures of the grown creatures, their eggs and, in the case of butterflies, their caterpillars. The process of identification will be even more rewarding if children are encouraged to keep notes of all their findings.

Providing Shelter
There are many ways of providing a good home for birds, animals and insects. For a start there are trees. If you already have trees in your garden treasure them and, if not, you should get planting right away – you can buy trees of varying ages. A good deciduous tree such as an oak, ash, beech or chestnut will play host to numerous birds and insects, not to mention squirrels. Of course these trees take a long time to grow but it is still worth planting them – just think that you are planting for generations of animals to come and try to make up in your own small way for all the wilful destruction that goes on every day. Natural woodland is so scarce that your trees will do a tremendous service. But don't forget to find out the eventual size of your tree and be careful to plant it with adequate space around. Children will also enjoy growing a little tree from an acorn or a chestnut (see Chapter 12). They may not succeed first time but it is definitely worth a try.

Unfortunately the trees that grow fastest, the Leyland cypress, are not as useful to birds and animals as the native deciduous trees with their great trunks and their nectar-filled flowers. But a hedge of cypress is a good place for birds to nest. Of the deciduous trees, the lovely silver birch are faster growing than most.

Fruit trees in time become a very good size and a mature apple or pear tree not only provides shelter but also a good deal of food for animals, birds and insects – red admiral butterflies are particularly fond of rotting apples. And in late summer the birds in our garden have a heavenly time feeding off the delicious berries of our mulberry tree.

Shrubs, both hedges and climbers, make wonderful homes for birds. The evergreens such as the ivy and berberis offer good cover in the early part of the year until the deciduous leaves appear in late spring to provide homes for the late arrivals.

Gerald Durrell described the old wall that surrounded his sunken garden as a rich hunting ground: 'There was a whole landscape on this wall if you peered close enough to see it' with its fungus, toadstools, ferns and moss. But even more exciting were the creatures for which it provided a refuge: 'The inhabitants of the wall were a mixed lot, and they were divided into day and night workers, the hunters and the hunted.' At night the hunters were the toads who fed on the many insects in the wall. By day 'it was more difficult to differentiate between the prey and the predators, for everything seemed to feed indiscriminately off everything else. Thus the hunting wasps searched out caterpillars and spiders; the spiders hunted for flies; the dragonflies, big, brittle, and hunting-pink, fed off the spiders and the flies; the swift, lithe, and multicoloured lizards fed off everything.' A dry English stone wall is every bit as exciting as Durrell's wall in Corfu and there are mice and birds joining the fun as well. So if you have such a wall, look after it.

Another invaluable home is a pile of rotting logs. Leave some for a while in your garden and in no time you will see that insects colonise. Then come the toads and snails for shelter, and the birds and hedgehogs that feed on the insects. And all kinds of interesting fungi and plant life will develop.

A BIRD GARDEN

There are two kinds of birds that will come to your garden: those who live in the same area all the year round and those who migrate either in summer or winter in search of warmer climates.

We all know the winter scene of the robin in the snow. He and the tits, finches, wrens, sparrows, starlings, thrushes and blackbirds, along

149

with many others, have to survive the cold winter. They have some canny methods of self-protection but you can help them by providing the right kind of food and shelter.

Then there are the swallows, swifts and house martins who thrill you in early summer when they return from warmer countries. These tend to be the birds which travel in flocks and it is amazing to see what a highly tuned sense of direction they have. The same swallow family may make their nests in the same eaves of a barn every year. Then, in late summer you see them lining up on the telegraph wires making a terrible racket – checking on their travellers cheques, passports and last-minute packing, I always feel. All at once at a given signal they are off to Italy, Spain, North Africa – anything to avoid the cold British winter. But at the same time there are birds from further north – the better-known examples being the fieldfare and the redwing – who winter in Britain.

Food

So, how can you welcome the birds throughout the year? In winter food, shelter and water are what they need. If you do not have a bird-table, either buy one or get building one right away – the simplest consists of no more than a tall post with a flat tray attached firmly on top. The point of having a bird-table rather than leaving the food on the ground or any other low flat surface is that you must protect the birds from their enemies, notably the household cat. While your bird-table should be in as sheltered a position as possible it should not be close to overhanging trees or fences from which a cat could spring. Also, place the table near enough to the house so that everyone can watch the fascinating goings on and note all the different species of birds.

Then, of course, you must protect the birds from each other. We have white fan-tailed pigeons living in an old dovecote and are very fond of them until they start chasing away the little birds whose needs may be greater than theirs. Our solution is to feed the pigeons on the ground and have a roof on the bird-table, so low that they cannot get under. Then there are those big bullies the starlings who make life difficult for the tits. The best answer to this problem is to hang some food on a piece of string from the table. Tits are very agile and will be able to cling on to this while having their meal whereas bigger, clumsier birds cannot. String bags of nuts are particularly popular with tits and you can also buy special containers for the nuts. We hang a bag of nuts just outside our kitchen window and the children are thrilled to watch the tiny birds feeding. We also attach a wire coat-hanger to the window with suction pads and hang titbits from it. Save those string bags that satsumas and oranges come in and fill them with bits of fat and other goodies such as crusts and old apples and hang them from the table. A half coconut is also a great success. If you feed the birds every day try to do it at the same time – breakfast is often the most convenient moment. Give breakfast scraps, nuts, biscuits, seed, bread, fat and lard, but remember to avoid fatty things and peanuts once the birds are feeding their young because they can be too rich for them. Make sure you provide food well into spring as this is the time when the young birds need most sustenance.

The other source of food is your garden. Birds love berries in winter, so trees like rowan, holly and hawthorn are a great success. Climbing cotoneaster, lovely, vivid pyracantha or firethorn, common ivy and berberis will all provide a rich feast. In the autumn you will find that your orchard fruit – the apples, pears and plums – are very popular with birds, though this is obviously a mixed blessing. Birds also love soft summer fruit which is why, since these are grown as your food, the fruit bushes should be surrounded by a bird-resistant cage.

Water

Like us, birds need water both to wash in and to drink. Ponds are not suitable because they are too deep and the birds risk drowning, but the old-fashioned bird-bath standing like a flattened bowl on a stem is ideal. You can make one for yourself using an old dustbin lid perhaps. In hard winters the water will freeze over and you must remember to crack the ice – a floating rubber ball will prevent it from icing over so easily. Whatever the weather you should always replace the dirty water regularly. Water seems much more essential in summer but, in fact, the birds will greatly appreciate a fresh bowl in winter when all around is frozen.

Nesting

Every spring the yew hedge which divides our garden is a hive of activity as the blackbirds get nesting – they actually seem to prefer living in gardens to anywhere else. We were also lucky enough to inherit some large old box bushes. Box grows very slowly but, with its dense foliage, it is a marvellously safe retreat for birds. Thick climbers like pyracantha and ivy also provide wonderful nesting sites for thrushes, finches and wrens. It's sensible to cut back these evergreen hedges and bushes in the autumn so the birds are not disturbed when they are nesting.

Evergreen hedges meet the needs of the resident birds. Then, come early summer, the migrants arrive and can make their nests among the new foliage of the non-evergreens such as clematis, particularly the thickly growing montana, Virginia creeper, Russian vine, the climbing *Hydrangea petiolaris*, wisteria and honeysuckle. Migrating birds like chiff-chaffs, spotted flycatchers, willow warblers, greenfinches and redstarts will all use these shrubs for their nests.

Other birds like tits and nuthatches nest in holes in old trees. These are getting fewer but you might think of providing an alternative in the form of a nesting-box. This should be attached very firmly to a piece of wood attached in turn to a tree trunk or a fence, out of reach of cats. It must be waterproof to protect the tiny birds inside and it must also be out of direct sunlight or once the weather warms up it could become a little oven and kill the inhabitants. It's important that the opening should only be 3cm ($1\frac{1}{8}$in) wide to stop invaders such as squirrels coming in and eating the eggs.

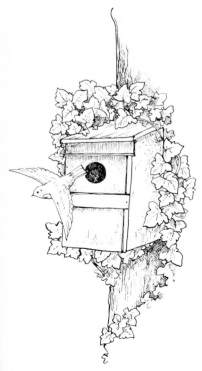

Put some inviting pieces of hay inside and then leave it undisturbed. Don't be too disappointed if nothing happens in the first or second year. You may have picked the wrong spot. But if, say, a tit does settle in and make a nest, you can peep in at intervals to see how the family is progressing. When the nest is made the female will lay her eggs and spend most of her time sitting on them, just disappearing at intervals to find food. Once the eggs have hatched both she and the male will spend a great deal of time searching for food for the fast-growing family.

Finally, they will all upsticks and fly away leaving you hoping that they will return next year. When they have finally gone, take down the box and give it a good clean using disinfectant and leave it in the sun to air out. Throw the nest away once you have examined it, then put the box back for next year. You will find this whole cycle of events quite fascinating.

You could also try and build a box which you could watch from inside the house. Build it against a window, giving it a false back which can be raised every now and again so you can see how the birds are getting on. Put this out of reach of very small children as they will not realise that by opening it too often you could frighten the birds away.

Swallows, swifts and house martins will build muddy-looking nests in the eaves of your roof. Don't remove them because the birds may well come back regularly if they think they are safely established there. They will arrive in early summer and for the next two months until they fly off with their young you will have a fascinating time watching them. They also love to nest in holes in walls so don't automatically fill them up.

YOUR BUTTERFLY AND INSECT GARDEN

'Butterfly' was one of the first long words my daughter learned as she sat in the sun watching them in pure delight. To me butterflies are like floating flowers and I can never have enough of them in the garden. I am also keen to attract bees and dragonflies and unusual beetles – in fact, the more interesting insects I can have, the better. What's more, many birds feed on the insects (but not on the butterflies) just as the insects feed on your plants so the wildlife in your garden is all very much related.

Butterflies naturally like a meadow with wild flowers and hedgerows, but modern farmers have seen to it that there are few hedgerows left and the insecticides used render many farm fields lethal. So, once again, your garden can be a refuge providing nectar from a mixture of cottage garden flowers and the wild flowers you allow to thrive there. The butterflies may not entirely take up residence because they like to flit about. Miriam Rothschild in her lovely book *The Butterfly Gardener* says she likes to imagine that butterflies think of her garden as a very good pub they can drop into whenever they wish.

Some butterflies live for a very short time – as little as two weeks – though some live much longer and some even hibernate through the winter. So, if you want to attract resident butterflies you should provide places where they can hibernate and later lay their eggs, and food for both the adult butterfly and the caterpillars.

153

The wonderfully bright greeny-yellow brimstone butterfly is the first to wake up in early spring from some hedge or hole in a wall and to me its appearance is the sure sign that spring is with us. There is not much nectar or pollen about to feed on at that time but catkins are a favourite food as are willow and sallow which often grow in old hedges and might be found in the wild part of your garden.

The most popular egg-laying site for a butterfly is a patch of stinging nettles, the bane of most gardeners who want only to get rid of them. While you don't want them growing everywhere, do let a clump go wild in a corner of the garden where they get a lot of sun as the butterflies' eggs need warmth to hatch.

Butterflies drink nectar from flowers and if you visit a large and wild garden in high summer it won't be difficult to see which flowers they like. Buddleia is such a favourite that it is often called the butterfly bush; there are many beautiful varieties, ranging from white to deep purple or orange flowers. Some have silvery leaves and I have one with yellow-edged leaves, so you can grow quite a selection, though they do take up a lot of space. Old-fashioned, sweet-smelling roses are also popular, and so are most flowers which are relatives of those they find in the wild – pansies, cornflowers, scabious, valerian, poppies, honeysuckle, large, flat-headed sedums and ornamental thistles will all be dotted with red admirals and peacocks vying for space with the bees. Put out a saucer of dilute syrup and you will have fun watching the butterflies drop by for a snack.

Most insects love herbs which have sweet-smelling flowers and butterflies, flies and bees will all hover around lavender hedges, catmint, rosemary and thyme. These herbs therefore serve a double purpose in your garden so it's worth putting a lot of space over to them. Another popular flower with most insects is the sunflower: they love its nectar and later the birds love its seeds. Better still, children love to grow them.

All insects need water so a shallow pond is useful. But failing that, just a plate of water or a small bird-bath will be a boon to them in times of great heat.

We know that butterflies and moths are attracted to flowers mostly by smell. This is particularly the case with moths at night. If you walk down a beautiful flower border in the evening you will notice that everything smells much stronger at that time and this is when the moths take over

from the butterflies. Some flowers, such as the beautiful tall, yellow evening primrose, only open up at night to attract moths. Night-scented stock give out strong smells in the evening and so do petunias, tobacco plants, honeysuckle and lovely pink or white valerian.

Moths are much less spectacular-looking than butterflies though some are extremely beautiful and very large indeed. There is much argument among experts about the reasons for the various markings on the wings of butterflies and moths. Some say that the bright butterfly colours are to match the flowers and so provide cover, while others believe that they serve as a warning to predators that butterflies taste horrible. Being night insects, moths don't need that bright colouring but many of them – and some butterflies – have spots on their backs which some experts say resemble eyes and therefore frighten predators.

Moths lay their eggs in various plants – such as lilac, poplar, privet and willow herb. These hatch out as caterpillars in summer then spend the winter below the soil. In spring they become chrysalises and then moths in time for the summer.

If you have planted the flowers that butterflies enjoy, the chances are that you will also attract many other insects including bees. With older children you might even consider keeping honey bees which require much less attention than most people think, but you should consult an expert before taking any action. This year we installed two hives in the corner of our garden and had nearly seventy pounds of honey in the first harvest. We built a high wire mesh-fence around so that the children cannot get too close but can still observe them and already my daughter goes off regularly to see how the bees are getting on. Honey bees love to eat herbs including lavender, catmint, sage and thyme, and so we are planting climbing roses and lavender around our hives, but in fact they will if necessary find their food from miles around: I have friends who keep hives on their roof in a London suburb with great success. In the first year we grew sweet peas up the wire which look stunning.

I thoroughly recommend reading one of the specialist books which will tell you all about the fascinating life of the honey bee colony.

Bumble bees are much larger. They also live in groups, but much smaller ones than the honey bee. I love to see these slow-moving creatures flying along the flower borders – sometimes you will find a huge, hairy backside

155

sticking up out of a foxglove or a lily flower. Foxgloves seem particularly popular with bumble bees which is fortunate as they are one of my favourite flowers .

THE WILD GARDEN POND

Ponds provide a wonderful focal point for wildlife. Birds and animals come to drink, frogs and toads come to breed and many snails, insects, worms and, of course, fish come to live there. As so many natural ponds in the countryside have now been drained these creatures need garden ponds more and more. The number of frogs is currently decreasing every year and you should do your best to put a stop to that.

If you do put in a pond, be sure that it's easily visible so you will know right away if anyone falls in. When I was very young we had a large duck pond beside the house. This was ideal because, unlike many ornamental ponds, it was very shallow at the edge so you could happily wade around in rubber boots and watch all the antics of the frogs and newts without falling in.

Today, with the help of special strong polythene which you can buy at garden centres, it is easy to lay a pond. First select your spot, making sure that trees do not overhang and that it gets quite a bit of sun. Then just dig out the shape you wish and line it with the polythene which should be cut much larger than the hole. Finally cover the edges of the polythene at the pool surround with stones. Remember to provide several levels to accommodate the different plants, reptiles and fish who will live there and be sure that there is a shallow area around the edge where small birds and animals can drink safely and bog-loving plants can thrive.

Many garden suppliers sell water plants. The most important are the pond weeds which produce the oxygen to keep the water fresh to stimulate pond life. Then, of course, there are many kinds of decorative flowers which you can grow to make it look extremely beautiful. The most obvious are water lilies which come in many lovely colours from white and yellow to shell pink and deep crimson. Be careful not to buy the large varieties which might completely take your pond over. Another pretty plant is the water hawthorn which floats on the surface and has a white, sweet-smelling

flower. At the sides of the pond in shallow water you can grow irises, marsh marigolds and rushes, but be sure not to grow the sort that will get too tall or spread too fast. Plant suppliers will advise you to plant the water plants in special baskets or pots, but if you are aiming for a fairly wild pool and don't mind the water not looking too clear, then put a layer of good earth about 15cm (6in) deep to settle on the bottom.

So what will live well in your pool? Firstly, you will be surprised how quickly many insects arrive unannounced, but to help this process along, go and fill a jam jar or bucket full of smelly sludge from an old ditch or pond nearby and put it gently into the pool. Within days you will see the results as different insects, beetles and snails make their appearance. Dragonflies will soon be laying their eggs and your pool will become a centre of life and have its own ecosystem going in no time at all.

Of course, the bigger the pool, the more life and bustle there will be. If it is fairly large you might keep a few fish such as (in Britain) sticklebacks or tiddlers, tench or rudd. If your pool is to be successful, it should not be overcrowded with any particular thing at the expense of others, so when you buy your fish, find out how many will be able to live in the pool you have. If you choose sticklebacks you will be fascinated to discover that they actually make nests for themselves when they are breeding. It is the father who does it and then protects the nest once the female has laid her eggs and gone away. When the eggs hatch he will nanny the shoal of tiny fish for some weeks till they can manage on their own.

Frogs, toads and newts may well choose to breed in your pond: lots did in ours. Frogs mate in the spring and, if you are lucky, you will hear their croaking mating calls. They lay the spawn to float on the surface of the pond (toads lay theirs in sort of ribbons tied around pond weed): we used to take a little, keep it in a jam jar with pond water and weed and watch as the little black dots in jelly developed arms, then legs. Eventually as they took on the shape of frogs we would put them back in the pond where they would leap about in the shallows.

If you are not lucky enough to attract frogs you can actually buy frog spawn. Ask your local pet shop. Remember that once the front legs appear the tadpole is nearly a frog and is therefore needing to eat insects rather than the algae in the water and in the weeds. In a pond nature will supply. In your house tiny pieces of raw meat should go down well instead.

ANIMALS

Finally your garden can be a home for wild animals, many of whom would normally live in the hedgerows but who are slowly being deprived of their natural homes. The most welcome of these is Mrs Tiggiwinkle the hedge-hog. Hedgehogs hunt at night eating slugs, worms, insects and snails: if you sit quietly in the garden you may hear them. They grunt and snuffle a lot which is why they got their pig-like name.

In mid-summer you might also be lucky enough to see the hedgehogs playing their very lively courtship games accompanied by lots of squeals and grunts. Babies are born about a month after mating. If you have a well-secluded hedge bottom the hedgehogs may make their home there and look after a litter of baby hedgehogs.

Other field animals that might turn up are field mice and harvest mice which can be distinguished from house mice by their brown fur. Harvest mice are tiny and in ideal circumstances make their nests among long corn stalks but modern farming methods, by causing the disappearance of so many of the hedgerows which are their natural home, have made these mice rather rare. Other very welcome garden animals are shrews, which look like tiny mice with deep brown fur and long, pointed noses. They live on worms, beetles and insects and, like the mice, their big enemy is your cat.

You hardly need to encourage grey squirrels into your garden: if there are trees with nuts, acorns or cones they will come of their own accord. The common grey squirrel was imported to England from North America and adapted to its new surroundings very quickly. The same was true in South Africa where, I am told, they were first imported as pets. They are great fun to watch as they leap among the trees and can become very tame, but they can also be very destructive, particularly when they eat birds' eggs. Sadly the smaller red squirrel is becoming very rare.

Unlike the squirrel most garden animals do their hunting and feeding at night. That is the only time that the mole will venture out, though you will of course know if you have moles because of the unpopular mounds they make in your lawn. Weasels are not likely to live in your garden but may come visiting at night as will foxes and even badgers. Often the only suggestion that they have been around is the footprints left behind.

Many people don't like bats: they are such odd-looking creatures and I was told when I was young that they get caught in your hair. This is not true. Sometimes at night a bat may fly into your bedroom and appear to panic. The thing to do is keep your light off and open the window wide. Bats make a high-pitched call which adults cannot hear though children can usually make it out. It is said to be part of the clever radar system they use to find their way about – the sound's echoes reflect back off the objects around them.

Bats tend to live in old barns or attics and the sheltered eaves of houses where they hang upside down and sleep by day. At night they head off catching insects as food as they fly. In some tropical countries you will find the famous vampire bats which I suppose gave bats their bad name, but those to be found in temperate climates such as the common bat, the pipistrel and the long-eared bat are quite harmless. If you want bats to stay you might make a bat-box which looks a bit like a bird-box but has its entry underneath. Bats naturally live in hollows in old trees but as these have declined in number, a few bat-boxes erected on trees around your garden may prove a boon to colonies of bats both for their daytime sleep and winter hibernation. They should be made of rough wood and not treated with anything as bats apparently hate strong smells.

YOUR NATURE DIARY

To really keep track of the natural developments in a garden children should keep a nature diary. This is something that I did from the age of eight. It's a wonderful way of keeping a record of what happened from year to year and great fun to do. There is no need to be methodical – just jot down notes: when you saw a fox track and what it looked like; when the first swallow arrived; when you put out your bird-table and who visited it. You can list when particular wild flowers came into bloom or the frog spawn developed legs and note the temperature: it will be interesting to compare the different rate at which things happen from year to year. It is always a good idea to have an outdoor thermometer and a rain gauge as well as children so enjoy reading them.

A looseleaf folder is better than a bound one as you may want to include bird feathers, bits of shells, insect skins, pressed flowers and twigs and stick in photos of birds' nests and birds which bulk it out. A magnifying glass is really useful for examining seeds, insects etc. in detail and later, of course, a microscope can provide incredible excitement as you find a whole new world revealed.

Gerald Durrell was encouraged to keep a nature diary by his first rather eccentric tutor George. 'At once,' he says, 'my enthusiastic but haphazard interest in nature became focused, for I found that by writing things down I could learn and remember much more. The only mornings that I was ever on time for my lessons were those which were given up to natural history.'

SAFETY IN THE GARDEN

'He did not see it happen, but the cracked bough must have begun to break at once, even at the first pressure of Hatty's slight weight. He heard the cracking, tearing sound; he heard Hatty's little "Oh!" of surprise that lasted only a part of a second before it became a scream, as she felt herself falling.'

TOM'S MIDNIGHT GARDEN

SAFETY IN THE GARDEN

YOUR garden can be a haven for your children but if you don't pay careful attention it can also be a place of danger, the scene of horrible accidents. Some things you will never be able to prevent – it is impossible, for instance, to stop a lively ten-year-old climbing trees. And there is nothing more irritating to a child than an overfussy parent nagging all the time. In a sense the garden should be a place where a child learns how to look after itself and it is important to instil a sense of trust in the older children by encouraging them to look after the younger ones. But most accidents can be prevented and it is worth giving thought to a list of the possible dangers. One important thing to remember is that every family should have a first-aid book. Make sure everyone knows where it lives – either in the medicine cupboard in the bathroom or in the kitchen – for when an accident happens speed is essential and a good first-aid book will tell you simply exactly what to do.

But back to prevention. To start with, see that your perimeter wall or fence is secure and that the gates shut properly. The gate latch should be high up so that small children cannot reach to open it – even better would be a child-proof lock – and any gaps in the fence should be firmly filled in to avoid toddlers wandering through. Many fences with cross slats are far too easy for children to climb over.

WATER

Water holds a great fascination for children from an early age but drowning is the third commonest cause of death in children. So, be enormously care-ful if you plan to have a pool or a pond of any sort, bearing in mind not just the age of your own children, but of children who may visit, because a tiny child can drown in just a few inches of water.

Paddling pools are a source of tremendous fun for children and the most popular variety with inflatable sides are very cheap. Be sure to empty them every evening and when they are not in use and never leave small children near them unattended. At eight months old my little boy hurtled across the lawn in his baby walker, hit the paddling pool and keeled over into it with the walker on top of him pinning him down with his head below the water. He could not even cry. Luckily I was close at hand and had him out in a brace of shakes. The walker was swiftly put in the attic. But if I had been at the other end of the garden it might have been too late. I still feel ill at the memory.

Garden ponds are more dangerous still because they are not emptied. If you have small children I would advise against installing one until they can swim and fend for themselves. If there is one in your garden already put a fence around it. Once the children are old enough to cope, the pond will prove a most exciting place as you will see in my chapter on wildlife.

Swimming pools should always have some kind of secure fencing around them and a lockable gate, even if your own children can swim. You could so easily have a visitor with a three-year-old who might roam there unknown to you with disastrous results.

Lastly water butts and tanks could prove lethal, so see that they always are securely covered.

TOOLS

Many garden tools are potentially deadly and should be used with the utmost care, particularly when children are around. The most dangerous of all is the lawn mower because to do its job well it must have sharp blades which revolve at great speed. Before mowing always be sure to remove any stones on the grass which might be sprayed out by the blades, and check that small children are indoors or well out of the way and under supervision. Never let a child come near a mower or drive it: many accidents have resulted from children being allowed to sit on mowers and tumbling off. Never use an electric mower when the grass is wet. Turn petrol mowers off when they are filled and be sure to store the petrol in a safe place. Never leave a mower with its engine on and, of course, unplug electric mowers when you are tinkering with them or whenever they are not actually in use.

With other electric tools like trimmers and hedge-cutters the same rules apply. Use them when children are not about and store them well out of reach.

But tools need not be electric to be dangerous. Many hand tools can do a lot of damage, particularly if left lying around. A toddler might innocently pierce his baby sister with a small fork and children of all ages could easily trip over forks, hoes or scythes, wounding themselves badly. The blades of a rake lying pointing upwards are especially dangerous.

Wounds inflicted in the garden need careful attention as so much dirt can get in, so if your child grazes himself even slightly in the garden always wash it right away with soap and clean water then treat with an antiseptic cream. In most countries children are injected against tetanus as a matter of course. See that yours are kept up regularly.

It is important, above all, that your garden shed has a good lock on it and is kept locked. It may be inconvenient for you, but children should not be allowed in at any point otherwise they are bound to use it as a place for hide-and-seek and perhaps harm themselves. As an additional precaution, all garden chemicals should be stored on a high shelf as children could obviously poison themselves by drinking them. Some chemicals can even do dreadful harm to their delicate skin.

POISONS

Most reputable chemical companies put warnings on their containers but obviously weedkillers, oils etc. should be kept well out of the way of curious little fingers. One extraordinarily stupid thing that adults often do is store poisonous liquids in apparently harmless bottles. I know someone who was seriously ill as a child when he drank wood preservative out of a cider bottle and doctors are full of similar stories of stupid adults using soft drink bottles to store lethal liquids.

If your child does take poison the chances are that you will find out in time to take action either because he tells you he feels ill – and he may develop symptoms such as vomiting, convulsions, retching or diarrhoea – or because you find the open bottle. Be sure to find out what he has eaten or drunk right away as he may lose consciousness. Get him to a doctor or the hospital remembering to take a sample of the poison with you. All the first-aid books insist that you should not try to make the child vomit.

POISONOUS PLANTS

Small children love picking and eating berries. Most berries like raspberries, elderberries and blackberries are, of course, totally harmless and also quite delicious so it stands to reason that they expect other berries to taste equally good. And this is where the great danger lies.

If you buy a book about poisonous plants you will find that some of your favourites like foxgloves and oleanders are poisonous but as children are highly unlikely to try and eat their leaves or roots there is almost no danger in growing them. However, do avoid planting things which produce an enticing-looking seed or berry which could literally – in the case of laburnum, monkshood or arum lilies – be fatal if eaten by an innocent toddler.

Here is a list of some of the commoner poisonous plants and weeds that you might find in your garden and which could prove dangerous.

I have included some which they are not likely to eat but could leave poison on their fingers if picked. Do always be sure that children wash their hands after playing in the garden and before eating a meal.

Common Monkshood (*Aconitum napellus*) This is a lovely, tall, blue delphinium-like flower which is grown in many gardens. Its tubers are fatally poisonous. The seeds and leaves can be too, though the poison is less concentrated, so don't grow it if you have small children.

Fools Parsley (*Aethusa cynapium*) This is a common weed in Europe and North America, often found in gardens. It can easily be mistaken for edible parsley, though only a child would make the mistake as it has white flowers and grows much larger.

Belladonna Lily (*Amaryllis belladonna*) This very beautiful flower is a native of South Africa but found in many North American and European gardens. The bulb is specially poisonous.

Columbine (*Aquilegia*) A lovely wild European plant which grows cultivated in gardens. The poison is not lethal but children should not eat the flowers.

Arum Lily (*Arum maculatum*) This grows in damp, woody areas of the garden. The red berries are very striking and can easily attract children. An overdose could kill a child.

Deadly Nightshade (*Atropa belladonna*) In Europe this grows wild but it has been introduced into America as a cultivated plant. The black berries can be fatal if eaten by children.

Autumn Crocus (*Colchicum*) These enchanting garden plants can be very dangerous to children who like to pick them. All parts of this plant are poisonous.

Hemlock (*Conium maculatum*) This tall, white flowering weed often grows near houses and in the wild areas of gardens. All parts of it are poisonous and can prove fatal, so clear it away if small children are using the area to play.

Lily of the Valley (*Convallaria majalis*) This lovely, sweet-smelling white flowering wood and garden plant contains poison in all parts. Children run the risk of severe illness if they are tempted to eat the red autumn berries.

Mezereon (*Daphne mezereum*) This is a very popular garden shrub producing a sweet-smelling pink flower in early spring. All parts of the plant are poisonous but it is the red berries which attract children and so can be dangerous.

Foxglove (*Digitalis purpurea*) The leaves of foxgloves are particularly poisonous but are unlikely to be dangerous as children are not tempted to eat them.

Spindle Tree (*Euonymus europaeus*) This tree is a popular garden plant because its berries are attractive but its bark, leaves and berries are poisonous. The berries can be fatal for children.

Spurge (*Euphorbia*) Many fascinating varieties of this plant are grown in gardens. All of them have a sticky white milk which drips from the stem when it is cut. It can inflame skin and seriously infect eyes if they are rubbed, so don't let children pick the plants.

Hellebore (*Helleborus*) All hellebores, particularly the Christmas rose, are popular winter flowering garden plants. Their stems and leaves can cause skin irritation and if children eat the seeds they may be very ill.

Golden Rain (*Laburnum*) This beautiful tree is grown widely in gardens in America and Europe. Its long, drooping clusters of yellow flowers in early summer give it the name golden rain. It is the seeds in long seed pods produced later in summer which contain poison. The effect can be fatal so don't plant such a tree if you have small children. If you inherit one, if it is a small tree you can remove the pods immediately they appear. If it's a large one be sure to rake them off the ground regularly.

Honeysuckle (*Lonicera*) Honeysuckle is a popular climbing plant grown widely in gardens. Its berries are poisonous and can cause horrible pains and vomiting if children eat them.

Oleander (*Nerium oleander*) These delightful shrubs are grown indoors in areas where there is sustained winter frost. Their leaves contain poison that can be lethal.

Solomon's Seal (*Polygonatum*) The berries of this interesting white flowering plant can cause poisoning if children eat them.

Rue (*Ruta*) This well-known herb contains a poison which can cause irritation to the skin when it is touched or picked. It should not therefore be grown near a play area.

Woody Nightshade (*Solanum dulcamara*) This is not so lethal as the deadly nightshade but once the purple and yellow flowers – which look like potato flowers – become berries they appeal to children who can be extremely ill if they eat them.

Yew (*Taxus baccata*) All parts of the yew are poisonous and children are frequently poisoned because they eat the berries, which contain very poisonous seeds, or chew the young shoots. A large enough dose can kill.

Mistletoe (*Viscum album*) As mistletoe grows high up in trees it is not likely to be eaten by small children. But remember that if you bring it into the house for Christmas decoration its berries might attract them and they are poisonous.

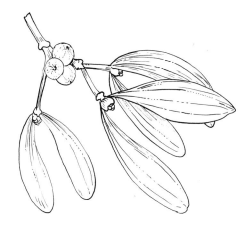

INDOOR JOBS FOR A RAINY DAY

'The next day the rain poured down in torrents again, and when Mary looked out of her window the moor was almost hidden by grey mist and cloud. There could be no going out today.'

THE SECRET GARDEN

INDOOR JOBS FOR A RAINY DAY

THE school holidays have arrived. You had all planned to spend the afternoon in the garden but the weather has different ideas – it is going to be far too cold and wet. But don't be disheartened. Grasp your opportunity. There are so many interesting things young gardeners can do indoors, particularly if parents are well-prepared with seeds, potting compost, jam jars, blotting paper, bulbs, pots, toothpicks and many other handy household articles which can be put to use. Obviously if you have a conservatory or porch there are any amount of things that can be started off and even grown to maturity indoors. But even with a sunny windowsill or a French window children can grow flowers or vegetables indoors and enjoy watching their progress at close quarters.

Before you begin, it is worth sitting comfortably. Working on the floor is never very satisfactory and things can easily get kicked over. When I was a child we had an old piece of oilcloth which went over the kitchen table on such occasions. Today, plastic is easy to get, but you will also need some old newspapers to work on. Then, depending on the time of year, you select your job. Most kitchen tables have a bright central light to work by which is a help.

GROWING FLOWERS AND VEGETABLES FROM SEED

This is quite a straightforward job for early spring but, with the exception of the simplest plants such as beans, it should be left to older children as the flowers need regular watering and should not be touched – something tiny children cannot resist. The transplanting process is a very delicate one but the advantage of indoor sowing is that you will have plants much earlier.

Let's take a very simple flower like a sweet pea which can be sown in winter or early spring. Its pea seeds are easy to handle and it grows well indoors. Take an old yogurt pot and make a hole in the bottom, then fill it to 0.5cm ($\frac{1}{4}$in) from the top with compost. Firm it down well with your fingers, plant 3 or 4 seeds 1cm ($\frac{1}{2}$in) deep, well spaced apart, and water liberally. Put the pot on an old saucer so that the earth does not damage your paint surfaces and place it on a windowsill or somewhere light. See that the soil always stays moist but does not get overwatered. Soon little shoots will appear. Once they are about 12.5cm (5in) high they can be transferred either to a bed outside if the frosts are past, or each to a single larger pot. When you transfer, remove all the soil gently from the yogurt pot and take the seedlings with the soil and the roots so the roots don't get destroyed. Vegetables like beans can also be grown this way. If you live in a flat or apartment without a garden sweet peas can look lovely in a tub indoors trained up around the window. If you remove the pods regularly, they will bloom for several months.

Growing a tomato plant

A rather more delicate seed is a tomato. The instructions for this would apply to many smaller seeds. You might start the seed either in a yogurt pot or in a seed tray: fill the tray with compost, firm it down, sit the tray in a bowl of cool water so the compost becomes saturated, then let it stand on thick newspaper or a draining board to drain a little. Sow the seeds 2.5cm (1in) apart and cover them with a very thin layer of compost. Put the tray in a light, warm place and water them regularly with a watering can that has a fine rose (i.e. tiny holes which make a very fine spray).

Once the seedlings are about 2.5cm (1in) tall you can transfer them to individual pots. Never touch the stem of a seedling when you move it. Hold one of its two leaves delicately and dig it up gently with a pencil or dibber trying to keep as much soil with the root as possible.

Tomatoes can be grown indoors or out and are extremely satisfying. The small bush varieties, such as 'Pixie', which produce tiny sweet tomatoes are particularly appealing to children.

Growing a broad bean in a jar

This is an age-old but endlessly fascinating way to demonstrate how a seed grows. In Chapter 4, How Does Your Garden Grow?, I tell a bit of the story, but to believe children must see for themselves. Your equipment is a jam jar, some blotting paper and a broad bean seed.

Roll the paper in a cylinder so it fits into the jam jar. Pour in an inch or so of water to dampen the blotting paper, then wedge the bean seed between the paper and the edge of the bottle about halfway up. Leave it in a cool dark place and within days the root will begin to appear — roots always come first — and grow down towards the water. Keep the water at the bottom so the paper cannot dry out. Soon the upper shoot will appear and grow upwards. At this point you can pot it up in a plant pot filled with compost and watch it grow into a big plant. To become a good-sized plant it will have to be transferred outside as beans are hearty feeders.

Games with mustard and cress

Mustard and cress are one of the fastest growing seeds. What's more, they require no feeding so can root in damp face cloths, kitchen paper or blotting paper very happily. They are very satisfying because of the quick results and are great fun to grow in shapes.

Put treble-thickness kitchen paper on an old tray or plate. Draw the shape you want — a train, a cat, a house, a child's name. Then damp it thoroughly, sow the seeds in the shape you have drawn and put the tray out of reach, bringing it down to examine each day. You won't have to wait long.

Then try growing mustard and cress in a yogurt pot full of damp kitchen paper. Put sticky plain paper round the pot and paint a face on it. When the seeds grow it looks like hair and can be trimmed.

Mustard and cress can also be made to sprout out of other vegetables. The obvious choices are vegetables that hold a lot of water such as marrows, pumpkins and potatoes. You can make a pumpkin face and dig small holes in the head where you plant the seeds. Soon it will look like hair.

Other seeds you can try this with are lentils which sprout very quickly indeed. However, they don't taste so delicious in sandwiches or salads as do mustard and cress.

Sprouting beans

Bean sprouts are easy to grow in a water-filled bottle and they are delicious.

Again, this is a quick and easy way to show small children how a seed develops. They don't need much light and will be ready in 3 or 4 days. Use mung beans, chick peas or alfalfa. Wash and soak them overnight, then put two tablespoons in a jam jar. Fill with water, then drain it away. Repeat this daily till they are well sprouted.

Peppers and aubergines (egg plants)
Both peppers and aubergines (often called egg plants) make extremely attractive indoor plants and are ideal to grow from seed and keep in tubs indoors so long as they have sun and warmth. You will need to feed them quite regularly with a liquid feed in order to get vegetables of any size. But all this is great fun for children as long as the feeding process is supervised.

Sow and grow the seeds just as the tomato. They may need staking. Nip out the growing tip of the plant when it is 10cm (4in) or so high so that it bushes out and does not get too tall.

Climbing French beans or runner beans
You can grow quite a crop of these indoors and harvest them months earlier than their outdoor cousins, but they will need staking in a large pot. Follow the instructions as for sweet peas but remember that the vegetables will need regular feeding if you are to get a sizable crop. Otherwise they are just very attractive to grow for their flowers and greenery. Be sure the windows are open and that the insects can get in to pollinate at flowering time.

GROWING BULBS

In *The Secret Garden* it was the first sight of the bulbs coming up that told Mary it was spring, and it was also what she found so exciting about the garden. Bulbs always have this cheering effect and they are easy enough for any child to grow. If you grow bulbs in compost in a pot one year you can plant them out in your garden once they die back and they will then divide and spread.

In chapters 5 and 9 I talk about the number of tiny bulbs you can grow.

178

They should all have a cool period outdoors after planting in pots and should be brought indoors again when they begin to sprout. A good idea when planting a group of bulbs of the same variety – say daffodils – is to plant them at different levels in the pot so they don't all grow to the same height.

Another unusual and attractive way of growing small bulbs is in 'crocus' pots. These are round pots with little holes in the side into which bulbs are planted. The effect is delightful.

The most entertaining way to demonstrate to children how a bulb grows is to grow a hyacinth bulb in a bulb glass, a tall glass with a thin neck and a wide rim on which the bulb sits with its bottom in the water. A thin-necked jam jar can be equally effective. Taking up water through its roots, the bulb sprouts and eventually flowers – an exciting process to watch. The one snag is that because the plant is only getting water and no food it is using up its food supply without replacing it and will not produce such a good flower the following year.

FRUIT TREES FROM PIPS AND SCRAPS

Getting something for nothing is always rewarding and the idea of getting a whole avocado tree or an orange tree from the stone or pips you were about to throw out quite takes your breath away. As it is really quite easy to do, this is an activity you will enjoy whether you have a garden or not. But unless you live in a Mediterranean climate these are indoor plants.

Avocados

Let's start with this increasingly popular fruit which comes in two shapes: one is rounded and is generally called the Guatemalan or Californian avocado while the other, which is more pear-shaped, is the Israeli or Florida version. The pear-shaped kind is easier to grow. Take the stone and give it a wash in tepid water (some people recommend soaking it in tepid water for 2 days). Fill a jam jar full of water and then balance the stone on the top by piercing it with several toothpicks. The flat end of the stone should be immersed in 0.5cm ($\frac{1}{4}$in) water. Then put it in a warm, darkish place – around 21°C (70°F) – and watch and wait, seeing that the water level is kept up. This waiting period can last many weeks or only one. But eventually the stone should crack up the middle and soon a root will emerge, followed some weeks later by an upward-growing shoot. If the water goes cloudy and no growth occurs then throw your stone away and start again.

The plant can be transferred to a plant pot filled with compost when the root system has developed to quite a good size. When the main shoot of the plant reaches 15cm (6in) or so snip it off at the top. This will enable the plant to grow outwards and become bushy. If the plant grows fast it should be transferred to a larger pot. Water it regularly and feed it periodically with liquid fertiliser and you should have a good-sized plant which will live in normal house temperatures, look very attractive and be the pride of the young person who started it off.

Oranges and lemons

All citrus fruits make the most charming little indoor trees and although they are unlikely to produce fruit like the original ones you eat, that hardly matters. Select some pips and plant three or four together in a pot of moist compost placing them 2.5cm (1in) apart and 1cm ($\frac{1}{2}$in) deep. Put the pot in a warm dark place. Once the shoots appear in 3–4 weeks' time, bring it into the light and when they get about 7.5cm (3in) tall they should be repotted separately into larger pots. Once they become little bushes they can live outside in summer on the terrace, balcony or windowsill. But at the slightest suggestion of frost they should be brought inside again. If you have some large houseplant in a big tub the children might like to plant their orange or tangerine pips in the surrounding earth and then transplant them later if anything comes up.

Apples, plums, pears, chestnuts, acorns . . .

These deciduous trees can all be started in pots from seeds and children will get great satisfaction from seeing a conker or an acorn become a small tree. But, of course, none of them make good houseplants and should be planted outside once they have become 30cm (1ft) tall. Remember that coming from countries that have a cold winter these seeds expect a cold spell after they drop from the tree. So when the pocketful of conkers or acorns is emptied out in early autumn, plant several in pots of compost with a slight covering of soil and then leave them outside to overwinter. In early spring bring them indoors and they will race ahead of their relatives outside. When the little plants appear put them into separate pots.

Pineapples

Pineapple tops can become the most striking houseplants. They are, in fact, bromeliads and their relatives of the same name are well-known house-plants. When you cut the top off the pineapple, leave quite a thick fleshy bit underneath. Let it dry for a day or so, then choose a pot with ample space around the pineapple top for watering purposes and fill it with good seed or cutting compost, perhaps with some sand added. Put the pineapple top in place, covering the fleshy part with compost. Water it and place it in the warmest, lightest place you have. Keep watering it regularly. When the top starts producing new light green leaves you will know it has rooted. When it gets larger you can put it in a bigger pot but always keep it warm. Your chances of success will increase if you spray the plant with water or place a propagator or polythene bag over its head making a mini-greenhouse. When the plant is a good size it may even produce baby pineapples.

Carrot tops, beetroot tops, parsnip tops

These do not make spectacular long-lasting plants like pineapples but you can create a delightful little garden on a plate or in a pot out of these kitchen scraps. Use large, fresh specimens and cut the carrot, beetroot or parsnip at least 1cm ($\frac{1}{2}$in) in from the end so there is quite a bit of flesh left as a base for the sprouting leaves. Then put the tops either on some compost in a tub or bowl with the compost just covering the base or in some shallow water on a plate. Water the compost then leave in a warmish, light place and the vegetables should begin to sprout in no time.

TAKING CUTTINGS

Some plants grow very easily from cuttings and so are fun for children to try out. The obvious ones are houseplants like tradescantia (wandering Jew) or pot plants like impatiens (busy Lizzie) and geraniums (pelargoniums). But most flowers with a fleshy stem will produce a root system quite quickly. You can buy special rooting powder which speeds up the process but with the easy plants I don't think it is worthwhile. All you need is a pot, some compost, some sand (not builders' sand) and a polythene bag or – better still – a propagator.

Take a side shoot of your plant – say busy Lizzie. It should be quite mature but not to the extent that it has developed a hard outside. Either snap it off cleanly or cut it about 7.5cm (3in) long. Strip the lower leaves from the bottom of the stem leaving 2.5cm (1in) clean. Your cutting is now ready for planting.

Mix your compost two thirds compost or peat to one third sand, place it in the pot and firm it down. Then take a pencil or a dibber, make a neat hole in the compost and slip the cutting 2.5cm (1in) deep into the hole and firm the compost round it. Water the cutting and place it in a warm, light place.

Most cuttings will take easily this way. But to make it even more likely you can make a little greenhouse by putting a polythene bag over its head. Take three sticks, place them at three corners of the pot and put the bag over the top. That way they act like tent poles stopping the bag from touching your cutting. Cut a few holes in the bag to let a little air in.

A really good, experienced gardener does not waste money buying new plants if he can get them elsewhere. Once you know about taking cuttings a whole world opens to you. You can admire a friend's rare bush and they will be delighted to give you a cutting or two to start up your own. Sharing plants is a very enjoyable link to have with friends and a child who learns this and many other basic skills now will enjoy them for a lifetime.

YOUR GARDEN CALENDAR

SPRING

* Dig your garden over to let the earth breathe.

* Remove all weeds.

* Add good compost to the soil.

* Sow the first hardy annual flower seeds.

* Sow half-hardy annuals indoors.

* Sow your first vegetable seeds of radish, carrot, lettuce, spring onions, herbs etc.

* Once the seedlings start appearing weed the soil.

* Water regularly to ensure the ground does not get dry.

* Prune roses before they begin to sprout.

SUMMER

* As the days get hotter be sure to water plants if it has not rained.

* Keep weeding around young plants.

* Buy bedding plants of half-hardy annuals or plant out the ones you sowed yourself.

* As flowers get tall stake them with sticks.

* Only move plants when the soil is damp and be careful to move some earth attached to the roots.

* Harvest your first vegetables.

* Grow bean plants up poles.

* Plant vegetable seeds in succession so you don't have them all ready at once.

* Grow bush tomatoes in ground or in tubs.

AUTUMN

* In a new garden, dig over the soil removing the weeds
  and leave it loosely dug.

* In an established garden annual flowers may bloom on
  well into autumn if you keep deadheading them.

* When the first frosts come the annuals will look dejected
  so pull them out and throw them on to the compost heap.

* Dig over the soil where your flowers and vegetables have
  been. Add compost or manure and leave it to weather.

* Take seed pods from your favourite plants to sow the seeds
  in spring. Store them in a dry, cool, dark place.

  * If you have grown everlasting flowers, it is time to make
    posies for winter decoration.

  * Plant wallflowers and forget-me-nots to flower with bulbs
    in spring.

WINTER

* This is the time to make plans.

* Make the design for your garden to plant in spring.

* You can now map out the space and lay any paths you want.

* See your tools are all in good order for the spring.

* Order the seed packets for spring sowing. (Consult with your friends about seed sharing.)

* Towards the end of winter sow the seeds of half-hardy annuals in trays or pots indoors.

* Protect more tender plants against frost using straw, sacking or old newspaper.

* On mild days plant trees, shrubs and roses.

BIBLIOGRAPHY

Burnett, Frances Hodgson, *The Secret Garden*, Heinemann, London, 1911

Carpenter, Humphrey and Prichard, Mari, *The Oxford Companion to Children's Literature*, Oxford University Press, Oxford, 1984

Carroll, Lewis, *Alice's Adventures in Wonderland*, Macmillan, London, 1865
Through the Looking Glass, Macmillan, London, 1871

Durrell, Gerald, *My Family and Other Animals*, Rupert Hart-Davis, London, 1956

Durrell, Gerald with Durrell, Lee, *The Amateur Naturalist*, Hamish Hamilton, London, 1982

Ewing, Julia Horatia, *A Flat Iron for a Farthing*, Bell and S., 1884
Mrs Overtheway's Remembrances, Bell and S., 1885

Grahame, Kenneth, *The Wind in the Willows*, Methuen, London, 1908

Jekyll, Gertrude, *Children and Gardens*, Newnes, London, 1908

Lutyens, Edwin, *The Letters of Edwin Lutyens*, Clare Percy and Jane Ridley (eds.), William Collins, London, 1985

Pearce, Phillipa, *Tom's Midnight Garden*, Oxford University Press, Oxford, 1958

Potter, Beatrix, *The Tale of Peter Rabbit*, Frederick Warne, London, 1902

Rothschild, Miriam and Farrell, Clive *The Butterfly Gardener*, Michael Joseph, London, 1983

Starý, František, *Poisonous Plants*, Hamlyn, London, 1983

Wilde, Oscar, 'The Selfish Giant' from *The Happy Prince and Other Tales*, Nutt, London, 1888

Wilson, Ron, *The Back Garden Wildlife Sanctuary Book*, Penguin, London, 1981

INDEX

achillea, 60
aconites, 85, 134
agar, experiments with, 68
ageratum, 92
alyssum, 82, 90, 92, 95
Anemone blanda, 134–5
animals in the garden, domestic, 26;
    wild, 159–60
annuals, half-hardy and hardy, 60;
    from seed, 76–7; suggested
    varieties of, 82–5
anthocyanins, 64
antirrhinum (snapdragon), 76, 80,
    82, 90, 97
arabis, 102
asters, 82, 92
aubrietia, 102
autumn in the garden, 81, 187

baby's breath (gypsophila), 83, 104
balcony gardens, 30–1
Bartram, John, 12
bats, 161
bees, bumble and honey, 155–6
begonias, 82, 92, 95
biennials, hardy, 60, 82–5
bird(s), 125–6, 145–8; attracting,
    147–8; -bath/table, 25, 150, 151;
    garden, 149–53; -scarers, 80–1
blue flax, 64
bluebells, 104

buddleia, 154
bulbs, 59, 122, 178–9; miniature,
    134–5; planting, 75, 134; sug-
    gested varieties of, 85–6
Burnett, F. H., *The Secret Garden*, 7,
    10, 115, 117–26, 173, 178
busy Lizzie (impatiens), 76, 83, 90,
    92, 183–4
butterflies, 145, 149
butterfly garden, 153–5

cacti and succulents, 138–9
calendar, garden, 185–8
campanula, 104
candytuft, 60, 76, 82, 92, 102, 104
Canterbury bells, 104
Carroll, Lewis, *Alice in Wonderland*,
    10, 90; Alice in Wonderland
    garden, 90–2; *Through the Looking
    Glass*, 51
cells, plant, 67
chemicals, manmade, use of, 147–8;
    dangers for children, 167–8;
    needed by plants, 55
children's gardens, colour schemes,
    122–5; planning, 73–4, 89; types
    of, 19–20, 89–104, 105–14, 129–42
chionodoxa, 75, 85, 135
chromatography, 64
colours of plants, 64
colour schemes, 122–5

compost, 54–5
cordyline, 100
crocuses, 75, 85, 92, 122, 134, 170
crop rotation, 77, 79
cuttings, 59, 183–4

daffodils, 59, 86, 92, 122, 134
dahlias, 82
digging, 74
digitalis (foxglove), 83, 104, 156, 170
division of plants, 59
Durrell, Gerald, *The Amateur
    Naturalist*, 146, 149, 162; *My
    Family and Other Animals*, 127,
    143

earthworms, 54, 66
everlasting flowers (helichrysum),
    76, 83
Ewing, J. H., *A Flat Iron for a Far-
    thing*, 12, 69; *Mrs Overtheway's
    Remembrances*, 15
experiments for children, 63–8,
    176–8

Fastia japonica, 100
fertilisers, 55–6
flowers, botanical descriptions of,
    62; from seeds, 76–7, 175–8; sug-
    gested varieties of, 82–5, 120–1,
    123–5; *see also* individual flowers

forget-me-nots (myosotis), 60, 81, 83
Forrest, George, 12
fountains, 25
foxgloves (digitalis), 83, 104, 156, 170
frogs, 158
fruit, 125; trees from seed, 180–3
fungal garden, 63

garden plans, family, American, 46–7; balcony, 30–1; large, 44–5; new, 38–9; patio, 32–3; paved, 34–5; suburban, small, 42–3; town, 34–7, 40–1; *see also* children's gardens
geraniums, 59, 183
glycerine as preservative, 67
grafting, 60
Grahame, Kenneth, *Wind in the Willows*, 95; Wind in the Willows garden, 95–7
grape hyacinth (muscari), 75, 86, 92, 135
gravity and seeds, 66
greenhouse, mini-, 63
gypsophila (baby's breath), 83, 104

half-hardy/hardy annuals, 60; *see also* annuals, biennials, perennials
hammocks, 21
heathers, 81
hedgehogs, 147, 159
hedges, 20, 25–6, 119, 145, 149
helichrysum (everlasting flower), 76, 83
herbs, 97; sowing, 77; suggestions, 98, 120, 137–8
HA/HHA/HB/HP *see* half-hardy/ hardy annuals
Hidcote, 122
hollyhocks, 104
honeysuckle, 154, 155, 171
houseplant gardens, 140–2

humus, 53, 54–5
hyacinths, 59, 85, 179

impatiens (busy Lizzie), 76, 83, 90, 92, 183–4
insects, attracting, 145–9, 153–6
Iris reticulata, 75, 85, 122, 135

Jekyll, Gertrude, *Children and Gardens*, 71, 74, 87, 89

lavender, 97, 154
lawns for children, 18–19
leaves, botanical description of, 62
light and plants, 56–7, 67
limnanthes (poached egg plant), 83
lobelia, 83, 90, 95
love-in-a-mist (nigella), 76, 80, 84, 104
Lutyens, Edwin, *The Letters of Edwin Lutyens*, 105

marigolds, 70, 83, 92, 95
mesembryanthemum, 83
Michaelmas daisies, 60
miniature gardens, 129–42
moles, 159
moths, 154–5
mowing, dangers for children from, 73–4
mulching, 79
muscari (grape hyacinth), 75, 86, 92, 135
myosotis (forget-me-not), 60, 81, 83

names, botanical, 62
narcissus, 86, 104, 134
nasturtium, 76, 83, 97, 104
nature diary, 161–2
nettles, stinging, 64
new gardens and children, 38–9
nicotiana (tobacco plant), 60, 76, 84, 97, 155

nigella (love-in-a-mist), 76, 80, 84, 104
nymphaea (water lily), 108

ornaments, garden, 25–6, 89–90, 94
osmosis, 67

paddling pools, 24–5, 166
pansies, 84, 97, 154
patios/terraces for children, 17–18, 32–3
paved gardens, 34–5
Pearce, Philippa, *Tom's Midnight Garden*, 10, 27
pelargoniums, 59, 183
perennials, hardy, 60; suggested varieties of, 82–5
pests, 66, 80, 147–8
petunias, 60, 76, 84, 90, 155
photosynthesis, 56–7, 64
pH testing, 56, 64
planning a child's garden, 73–4, 89–104
plans for family gardens, 29–48
play places, 20–2
poached egg plant (limnanthes), 83
poisonous plants, 168–72
ponds, 25, 90, 156–8, 165–6
poppies, 84, 104, 154
Potter, Beatrix, *The Tale of Peter Rabbit*, 92; Mr McGregor's Garden, 92–4
primroses, 84, 155
pruning, 61

reproduction, plant, 58–60
rhizomes, division of, 59
rock plants, 130–2
roots, function of, 57–8, 66
root stock, 60
roses, 61, 75, 90, 154; climbing, 119–20, 123; floribunda, 104; miniature, 104, 120, 132–3; planting, 75; pruning, 61; rambler, 120; suggested varieties of, 119–20

Rothschild, M. & Farrell, C., *The Butterfly Gardener*, 153
rudbeckia, 84, 108
runners, 59

sandpits, 21, 29
saxifrages, 102
scillas, 75, 86, 92, 104, 122, 135
seeds, 58–9, 61; flowers and and vegetables, from, 76–7, 92–4, 175–8; fruit trees, from, 180–3; production by plants of, 80
see-saws, 22
shrews, 159
shrubs, 75, 149
Sissinghurst, 122
slides, 22, 24
snapdragons (antirrhinum), 76, 80, 82, 97
snowdrops, 75, 104, 122, 134
soil, composition and types of, 53–7, 66; mulching, 79
spore prints, 67
squirrels, 159
stakes, 79

Stevenson, R. L., 'My Kingdom', 106
stocks, 84, 155
succulent plants, 138–9
sundials, 25
sunflowers, 76, 84, 95, 104
sweetpeas, 76, 85
swimming pools, plastic, 25
swings, 21

terrariums, 141–2
toads, 158
tobacco plants (nicotiana), 60, 76, 84, 97, 155
tools, 71–3; dangers for children from, 166–7
topiary, 25–6
town gardens, 36–7, 40–1
tradescantia (wandering Jew), 183
transpiration, 63
tray gardens, 129
trees, 148–9
troughs and tubs, 130
tulips, 59, 75, 86, 92, 95, 134
tunnels, 24

valerian, 154, 155
vegetables, from seed, 77, 92–4, 175–8
vernalisation, 56

wallflowers, 60, 81
wandering Jew (tradescantia), 183
WATCH, children's conservation group, 108, 146–7
water, dangers for children from, 165–6
water and plants, 57, 63
weeds, 61–2 , 79
wendy houses, 18, 24, 73
Where the Wild Things Are, 100; Wild Things garden, 100–2
Wilde, Oscar, 'The Selfish Giant', 9
wild flowers, 100
wildlife, attracting, 145–61; garden plan, 48–50

yucca, 100

zinnias, 85, 92